ABOUT THE AUTHOR

Caitriona Coyle was born and reared in Co. Donegal, Ireland; she has however lived in Dublin for most of her adult life.

She taught English and Religion for 30 years in a suburban Dublin school taking early retirement in 2012 to concentrate on her own writing. These days she divides her time between her native Donegal and Dublin. Caitriona is married and has two grown up daughters.

DEDICATION

To Patti and Terri…just because

Caitriona Coyle

COLLEGE GIRLS

Leabharlanna Poiblí Chathair Baile Átha Cliath

Dublin City Public Libraries

AUSTIN MACAULEY
PUBLISHERS LTD.

A CIP catalogue record for this title is available from the British Library.

ISBN 9781786930576 (Paperback)
ISBN 9781786930583 (Hardback)
ISBN 9781786930590 (E-Book)
www.austinmacauley.com

First Published (2017)
Austin Macauley Publishers Ltd.
25 Canada Square
Canary Wharf
London
E14 5LQ

ACKNOWLEDGMENTS

Love and thanks to my stalwart friend Frances Roberts who listened to every chapter as I wrote, offering me fierce and wonderful encouragement. To my husband Frank, thanks for believing in me and never doubting for a moment that I could write; much love. To Kate and Holly, my beautiful girls, for their patience when I constantly pestered them for help with the 'computer stuff', again much love.

A shoutout also to my writing buddies who attended the Big Smoke writing factory with me and were a great help and support in workshopping the early chapters.

She walked up the stairs in front of me. The hostel floorboards creaked and her strawberry blonde hair swished from side to side, skimming the top of her bum. When we reached our cells she turned around and I was comforted to see that she wasn't extremely pretty. As my envy dissipated I absorbed her sharp features and piercing eyes. She took me in at a glance, judging me, even a little suspicious of me. Her mouth was not quick to smile but when she spoke she seemed pleasant enough.

I was happy to chat to her and I suspect she was glad of my company too. As we talked we discovered that we were both heading to the same college, which helped to assuage my sense of isolation. I was from Donegal, she was from West Cork, both fresh out of boarding school and eager for adventure. I'm not sure looking back whether I needed her more than she needed me then, but I have a sneaky suspicion that I was more insecure.

We took to college like cats to water, running out of the main doors every day at lunchtime, invariably finding ourselves wandering around O'Connell Street or down Henry Street. We killed time in coffee shops or mooched about in department stores like Arnotts, Clerys, handling goods we couldn't afford. I certainly didn't have the money to purchase the glorious clothes that made my mouth water with longing. Ethna's funds were healthier than mine but not in an obvious way. Now and again she would treat us to cake with the coffees, even rising to evening tea in Pizzaland, which I adored.

As it turned out, there were ten girls in the hostel in Henrietta Street all going to the same college. We walked up in a pack every morning and ran back like lunatics from the pub up the street every evening. The nuns locked the doors at 11 o'clock at night and like Cinderellas we had to leave McGowan's just as the craic was getting good.

After one week Ethna and I decided we couldn't stick the hostel any longer. Five years of boarding school had left us with a low tolerance for mass-produced food and regimental rules like lights out and no talking in the dormitories after dark. To hell with that. We wanted to be free, live the dream, be in charge of our own schedules. I already had my eye on a few fellas in the pub but I knew I couldn't bring anyone back to a hostel.

It was Dublin 1978 and we wanted to be liberated. A 60's vibe permeated the social scene then. Dublin was a village filled with cool people in torn jeans and grandfather shirts and wee Cathy Logue from Donegal yearned to be one of them. The smell of dope hung in the air as Bad Company's "Feel like Making Love" floated out from record stores. Bohemian guys in velvet jackets and flares swaggered along the streets with Led Zeppelin or Jethro Tull albums tucked ostentatiously under their oxters. Yes, Dublin was a village, Greenwich Village and I wanted to be the neat girl sitting cross-legged at parties passing along the joint and swaying dreamily to a Joni Mitchell song. Perhaps Ethna Mullins from West Cork didn't quite share my enthusiasm for wearing flowers in her hair but she kept her reticence in check as we began our search for a new home.

We had only viewed one or two flats when Maeve McLaughlin rang me at the hostel. She was a friend from home who had been a few years ahead of me in boarding school and the lease on her accommodation was up. I was delighted she wanted to move in with us and she took my word for it that Ethna was easy enough company.

"I hope you don't mind" I said as we walked up to college the following day. "We'll probably get a bigger flat between three of us, might work out cheaper too".

"What's Maeve like?" green probing eyes looked at me.

"Maeve is lovely" I said. She is tall and willowy with shoulder length auburn hair and beautiful brown eyes. People often say she looks more Spanish than Irish. She's good craic too and really intelligent. I know you'll like her."

The following afternoon we met under Clery's Clock eager to begin our search. Maeve was relaxed and friendly as I introduced her to Ethna and I felt a surge of warmth and excitement as we pressed our heads together over the Evening Press. Maeve was in third year in U.C.D. which was on the opposite side of town so we had to narrow our search to areas that would suit all of us.

"You know Dublin better than us Maeve" I said. "Where do you suggest we look?"

"We should concentrate on Rathmines, Rathgar and around South Circular Road".

"Rathmines!" I said, "Is that place not full of smeara dubha?"

"That's blackberries in English isn't it?" asked Ethna, rather bemused.

"It is indeed" said Maeve. "That's our wee code for black people Ethna."

Maeve and I laughed in a low scheming way and Ethna smiled, watching the pair of us, knowing she would have to come to par quickly.

We looked at some depressing places over the next few days but we viewed gorgeous flats too with central heating and separate bedrooms which always seemed to be snapped up by three nurses or three bank clerks, leaving us feeling dejected and tired.

On the fifth day of our search we met Maeve outside Trinity and she was all business. "Listen" she said, "I found us a flat. I went out early today and for once I was the first to view this place on South Circular Road so I just went ahead and put down a deposit to hold it."

"What's it like?" I was excited.

"It's not fabulous by any means but it's got loads of character, with marble fireplaces and a big bay window in the bedroom."

"When can we see it?" Ethna didn't sound as excited.

"We can go right now. The landlord will be there to give us our keys at five o'clock." So, off we trundled to the 16 bus stop, glad we had the money in our pockets to pay the deposit and the first week's rent. We pestered Maeve with questions 'til we finally got to the front door of 91 South Circular Road.

Maeve rang the bell for Flat No. 1 and it opened to reveal a small, stocky man wearing a checked sports jacket and grey slacks. He looked about sixty and as he ushered us in my first though was 'dump!' There was a musty smell in the hallway and years of phone directories were piled in heaps along the corridor. Straight ahead was a staircase and inside the first door on the right hand side of the hall was our flat. Mr. Tommy Heenan didn't stand on ceremony. The rent was £10 per week. He would collect it every Saturday. He wrote our names and college numbers into a little red notebook and left us a card with his secretary's details. We were to ring her if we had any queries. We watched him through the bay window, driving off in his Mercedes; then we turned to inspect our new abode.

Maeve followed us with anxious eyes as we scanned the place, the burden of choosing it weighing on her shoulders. It certainly wasn't fabulous, but it had a certain diluted Victorian charm. Shabby furniture and faded carpet made it feel dusty and dreary, but it was ours. The reality of what that meant began to seep into our bones and disappointment gave way to hope.

"Well, what do yous think?" Maeve speaking slowly.

"It's not bad" Ethna's eyes still scrutinising.

"It has potential; we'll put our own stamp on it." I felt positive, throwing open the double doors into the bedroom. We had one bedroom with three single beds and three old fashioned free-standing wardrobes. The black marble fireplace gave it a touch of grandeur and we used the mantle as a shelf to hold our makeup and trinkets of jewellery.

The living room was furnished with a faded pink sofa and matching armchair, arranged in front of another imposing, veined marble fireplace with a large mirror over the mantle. There were mismatched pieces of furniture, a dilapidated sideboard, small table, two chairs, smaller table in the recess near the fireplace. An ancient looking turquoise two-bar heater sat waiting to be plugged in. There were no windows in the living room; a glass panelled door leading into the kitchen provided the only scrap of daylight.

The kitchen was really just a pantry with a stainless steel sink, a few wall cupboards and a cream coloured gas cooker that had seen better days. There were no nuns though and no bells and definitely no rules. We sat on the faded pink sofa and lit our cigarettes, exhaling slowly, luxuriously, feeling the delicious anticipation rising within us.

"Did yous see the bathroom yet?" Maeve asked. "It's down at the end of the hall. Go on and have a look." We raced down to the door marked WC and the smell of stale urine assaulted our nostrils.

"God this is rotten. I'll never use that bath," Ethna was adamant.

"You'd be dirtier getting out of that thing than you were getting into it" I laughed. It'll be the cat's lick at the kitchen sink for me". The front door slammed as we walked back towards our flat and we caught sight of a young woman about to mount the stairs. We were still laughing, determined not to let the unsavoury state of the bathroom dampen our spirits. She looked quickly at both of us as she placed her hand on the banister. We closed the door and threw ourselves down on the sofa, still giggling as Maeve rubbed her hands together gleefully, sharing our horror.

"This place is going to be a challenge" I said and I suddenly remembered the girl at the bottom of the stairs and the playful glint in her eyes.

We settled in and the flat began to look like a set from the Abbey. Colourful scarves hung from the bedroom fireplace with love-beads and leather purses bought at jumble sales and markets. Beer mats on the walls in the sitting room along with psychedelic posters of circles and flowers took the bare look off the place.

At first the noise from the street kept us awake at night but as the weeks passed we grew accustomed to the sounds of cars and sirens until we stopped hearing them altogether. We became familiar too with the internal noises of the house; the squeaking floorboards and slamming doors as the inhabitants in the other flats got on with their daily lives.

Ethna and I took the 16 bus across the city every morning and I decided we should never pay the full fare. The same bus conductors worked the route, getting to know their regular customers and their destinations. In the main they were good humoured fellows who sang as they doled out tickets, flirting with the women, spouting witticisms; even sharing cigarettes with us on occasion when it was quiet and the bus was almost deserted. Others though were moody and miserable, watching like hawks to see if we would disembark at our selected locations.

"Well ladies, where are we off to today?"

I would tell him we were going to O'Connell Street or Parnell Square, ignoring his sneering eyes, the aggressive way he handed us the tickets. We sat then; two frightened rabbits preparing to flee should an Inspector get on, because he would make us pay the full amount, publicly humiliating us with his inquisition. Most of the time we made it to Drumcondra, thrilled that we had hoodwinked C.I.E., on other occasions though, we had to scarper, Bugs Bunny style as a disgruntled conductor made a beeline for us. He would stand on the platform at the back of the bus, a fuming Elmer Fudd, as we laughed waving at him, hoping his shift would be over by the time we took the bus home.

College life took on a comfortable rhythm as we became familiar with our timetables, the layout of the building and the names of our lecturers. With only six lecture halls, a library and a canteen finding our bearings wasn't a problem. There were just 52 students in each year, so after our first week of introductions and orientation, we practically knew everyone in the class of '78.

Dublin students dominated, with most other counties being represented in small numbers. The city girls took trains across town from places we were unfamiliar with like Dalky or Enniskerry and they spoke with polished, confident voices. There were accents from Sligo, Kerry and Roscommon, with one girl from Tipperary speaking with such guttural ferocity I secretly vowed never to be left alone with her.

Judging by their clothes, they were in the main, a conventional bunch with midi-skirts, knee length boots and pretty blouses the order of the day. There were a few possible allies in the mix and we circled each other watchfully, waiting for the opportunity to make contact.

Most of the lecturers were middle-aged priests or nuns who dictated reams of notes, in monotone voices, attempting occasionally to ask intriguing questions.

"How do we know the Bible is inspired?" Or "What is the doctrine of Transubstantiation?" Clever geeks responded while most of us stared at the floor, feigning contemplation. The only class I enjoyed was English literature with Mr. Boyde, who always arrived late, smelling of whiskey and cigarettes. He invited us to smoke in his lectures as he rambled off script into all sorts of dangerous territory. In his beautiful plumy accent he would throw down the gauntlet; "Don't you lot know that Transubstantiation is cannibalism?"

Geek hackles rose as they rejected his theory which culminated in his declaration that we were all as 'thick as two short planks!' Faces were crimson with insult, hurt, outrage as I sat smirking, inhaling my cigarette, enjoying the entertainment. There were only six boys in the class of '78 and they left a lot to be desired.

"What do you think of the talent?" I asked Ethna one evening as we headed home on the bus. She looked at me as if it was a strange question, then realised I expected her to engage with gusto.

"They're okay, I suppose."

"Okay? Jesus they're far from okay, I never saw such a bunch of eejits in my life. Which one would you fancy now for example?"

"Joey's not bad looking and he seems to have a nice personality."

"Yeah well he's the best of a bad lot, but Lord did you ever see anything like Willie?"

"He's a mature student, he's older than us." Her voice sounded apologetic.

"Jesus the teeth are mature too. If they were any maturer they'd be down on his chest. And the Emmet fella looks like the umbilical cord was only cut yesterday. It'll be another couple of years before he starts to shave." I continued my uncharitable analyses until we reached our bus stop on South Circular just as darkness began to fall and the street lights came on.

The girl we had seen on our first night in the house was in the hall as we walked through; standing by the phone just inside the front door. She continued with her conversation but nodded at us, winking as we passed her by. She was wearing a red tricel polo neck with a black flared skirt and a black leather jacket. What was unusual was that she wasn't wearing any tights on that nippy October evening; her legs looked blue and cold while her bare feet disappeared into a pair of sensible looking black brogues. Maeve was already home, working on another assignment at the sitting room table, course books and notepads spread out around her. Ethna went straight to the kitchen while I sat down beside Maeve for a moment.

"We saw the girl from No. 2 in the hall just now" I said. "She seems friendly."

"She is" Maeve looked up from her work. "I got talking to her earlier on, her name is Rosie Diver."

My eyes widened; "Where is she from?"

"Limerick."

"Did you find out what she does?" A defiant tone in my voice.

"I was only talking to her for a few minutes. I did notice she was carrying a clipper-board though."

"She probably works in an office then, secretarial work I'd say," confident now that I had discovered her profession.

Over the next few weeks, on our comings and goings we bumped into Rosie in the hall or on the front steps until it seemed foolish not to stop for a little chat. She was delighted to hear Ethna was from West Cork, said she had cousins there and although I mentioned Letterkenny a few times she didn't specify which part of Limerick she was from. Probably in her mid-twenties I thought as I stood close to her noticing that she wasn't wearing any makeup or jewellery. Her eyes seemed old and experienced while her full lips moved sensuously when she spoke; her whole mouth tilting slightly to the left. She was heavy set, plump even, and as she moved toward the stairs, introductions over, I noticed she had a limp. Her right leg seemed shorter than her left, creating a waddle as she walked, causing her to land heavily on her right hip each step she took. Her black skirt rode up at the back in an ungainly fashion and it was apparent, obviously so, that the leather jacket had seen better days.

"She doesn't look like a secretary" Ethna suggested as we closed the flat door and flopped down on the musty pink sofa. "She looks more like she works in a supermarket or something; the clipper-board is for stocktaking I bet."

"I don't know," Maeve's eyes narrowed in that knowing, conspiratorial way they were wont to do. "It's hard to tell."

"Well we're bound to find out soon enough" I said. "Sure we told her that we're students, so there's no need for secrets."

The following evening as Maeve heated the beans and I buttered toast there was a gentle knock at the door, opening it we could hear Ethna saying "come in Rosie, not at all, you're not disturbing us one bit. Will you have a cup of tea?" There she sat in the pink armchair, Rosie from Limerick, totally relaxed despite the fact that her stout short legs were crossed in an awkward pose. We chatted comfortably as we ate our supper and she slurped noisily on her sweet tea. To our delight we found her quick witted and funny with turns of phrase she evidently enjoyed using as she joined us in gales of laughter and giggles that followed every little anecdote she amused us with, until she noticed the time and rose from the armchair to go.

"I suppose you women are strapped for cash," she said, "being students and all. If ye ever feel like making a few bob just let me know, the boss is always interested in taking on extra people."

I took courage in both hands, "What would we have to do, Rosie?"

"A bit of this and that, nothing too taxing," her eyes held mine, filled with innuendo.

We were silent as she mounted the stairs, till we heard her flat door slamming.

"She is some ticket!" Ethna exclaimed.

"We still don't know what she does." I looked at Maeve to see if she had any bright ideas. Her eyes wandered as she mused, "God only knows, whatever it is she doesn't make much money."

"She doesn't even wear tights," I almost squealed.

"Did you hear her advice about saving money on taxis?" Ethna looked at me, smirking "you think you're clever on the buses."

"They must all know her by now," Maeve rolled her eyes and we laughed, remembering what she told us about the stunt she pulled on a regular basis.

Work had begun on paving Grafton Street so Rosie knew the taxis could only drop her near Suffolk Street or Chatham Street. She would jump out when this happened and say "I ordered a taxi to Grafton Street and I still have to walk all the way to Switzers. Well you can fuck off if you think I'm paying for this!" She would slam the taxi door and go limpedy-limp down the poshest thoroughfare in Ireland and not one of those taxi men dared to follow her or insist she pay the fare.

"I'm just thinking" Maeve's eyes were narrowing again, "would she be employed by Switzers surveying punters about customer service?"

Ethna was indignant "dressed like that?"

"She should hang around the perfume counters a bit more" I sniffed, Ethna nodded vigorously. Maeve wasn't impressed, "Logue, you're a wee bitch."

"No, she's right," Ethna agreed, "I got it too." Maeve shrugged, turning back to her assignment as Ethna and I lit our cigarettes and took the weight off our feet, carefully avoiding the pink armchair.

Halloween was just around the corner, apparently the college hosted a fancy-dress party every year, before mid-term break. Ethna had unearthed a huge crimson cape on top of her wardrobe, left behind, we assumed, by a previous tenant. It looked like something one would wear during a secret meeting of the Freemasons and I couldn't wait to see how Ethna would use it. She emerged eventually in kakki shorts and shirt, shod in heavy mountain boots, the cape draped incongruously over her shoulders. She wore her hair in two golden plaits with her face made up like a ventriloquist's dummy. I had to do with dressing up as a farmer's wife, in a black skirt and wellingtons, making it humorous by stuffing two large towels down the front of my worn Aran cardigan, tying a piece of cord around my waist to accentuate my generous bust. I wore a head-scarf tied under my chin in a tight bow pursing my lips together suggesting a mouth devoid of teeth.

We went first to McGowan's, the pub nearest the college and the place was heaving with students in fancy dress as well as the local customers who appeared to be enjoying the spectacle. There was an unspoken liberation in the costumes making us loud and garrulous as we drank our pints of beer with abandon.

Willie came dressed as a pregnant Virgin Mary, sporting a sign saying "The Immaculate Conception." Joey was dressed as Hitler and he flirted with nuns in skimpy habits who flashed their suspenders and stockings, enjoying the irreverence of the occasion. The dairy farmers of Ireland had gone on strike that week and naively I had played into the hands of some smart asses who chortled and gloated as they caught sight of my assets.

"Jaysus boys" one of them announced, "would you look at this and a milk strike on!"

I monopolised the attention, throwing my shoulders back, protruding my generous bosom into as many conversations as possible, downing pints of Harp, trying to catch Joey's eye, without success. Across in college the disco ball sparkled, everyone dancing like dervishes, heads shaking, hair flying to Bob Seger's 'Hollywood Nights'.

Ethna's dance moves seemed out of kilter as she pounded the floor with mannish boots, the red taffeta cape undulating. Willie's pregnancy bump was dropping lower and lower and he licked his teeth heading in my direction. Billy Joel in the background singing 'she's always a woman to me'. Managing to give him the slip, I tried flirting with a fourth year student, asking him if he fancied a feel of my ample mammaries, gyrating seductively, pretending that my wellies weren't sticking to the floor.

Talent was thin on the ground though, with no fanciable outsiders manifesting in the course of the night, I grew weary, telling Ethna we should head out, try to get the last bus home.

"I fancy a burger or something," Ethna announced as we made our way onto Lower Drumcondra Road.

"Me too but I haven't enough money."

"We'll go over to the Perki Chick," she slurred and I followed her assuming she was going to treat me, as usual. A long queue had formed as we entered the chipper and without warning Ethna began to work the line asking each person if they could spare a few bob. I watched her, filled with admiration as she gathered up the price of two batter burgers and chips. The young Italian behind the counter asked us if we wanted "salt a' vinega'" and we howled laughing repeating "salt a' vinega'" over and over until we were halfway down Dorset Street, grease running down our chins; Ethna's cape blowing back in the wind. We walked all the way home oblivious to the pageant we presented, staggering up O'Connell Street, Ethna occasionally knocking her boots together in aggressive military fashion. By the time we reached 91 we were beyond exhaustion, flinging ourselves into the beds fully clothed, Ethna snoring like a banshee within seconds. I envied Maeve asleep and cosy with the prospect of waking rested and alert in the morning as the dull ache of hangover inveigled its way into my head.

Ethna took the train to Cork the next day, looking drawn and pale, mirroring my own hangdog face. Maeve and I took the bus to Donegal, a four hour journey that I made shorter regaling her with tales from the night before. She rubbed her hands in glee, incredulous that Ethna had the gall to beg for our supper.

"Jesus, yous won't be able to go in there again," she seemed to draw satisfaction from this.

"I'm sure they've seen worse" I laughed, the image of Ethna scrounging floated before my eyes making my headache bearable.

The week at home was tense. My mother quizzed me incessantly about the cheques I had written and the money I had spent. My father seemed displeased that I had moved out of the hostel and in with Maeve McLaughlin who 'wasn't near the mark' as far as he was concerned. As usual, he was drinking heavily, absent most of the time and she fretted and instigated rows on his return. When Sunday came around I was glad to pack my rucksack and take the bus back to Dublin and 91 South Circular.

Maeve enjoyed her time at home having met some cool fellas who played in a traditional band called 'Rustic'. She gave the lead singer our address telling him they were welcome to stay with us any time they had a gig in Dublin.

This cheered me a little despite the fact that the flat was freezing and we couldn't afford to buy coal. We made tea and sat on top of the two-bar heater trying to get warm, listening to the sounds in the hall; eventually hearing Ethna's key in the door. She looked pale and tired with eyes that suggested her week at home wasn't much better than mine.

On the bus the following morning she was quiet as I stared out the window listening to mum's voice in my head.

"You'll have to watch your spending. That man never gives me a penny you know," he prefers to throw it over counters. If I wasn't working we'd be out on the street."

As the bus turned onto Parnell Square Ethna looked at me; "It's my father's anniversary on Thursday, I'd like to get a mass said for him," she handed me a cigarette.

I knew he had died two years previously when she was just fifteen; had a massive heart-attack on his way home from the pub. Her mother found him lying in the ditch, the two brothers got him back to the house but he was dead by the time the ambulance arrived. She told me that the first night in the hostel and I needed to say something meaningful to her now. "We'll ask Fr. Weller today, he'll say a nice wee mass I'm sure" I ignored the welled up eyes, stubbing out my cigarette on the floor as the bus pulled into our stop.

We were only in the college two months but already we felt that Fr. Weller the college director had a soft spot for us. He would come down to the foyer occasionally looking for Ethna or myself, taking one of us gently by the elbow, up to his office for a nice little chat.

"How are you settling in Cathy?" big warm smile.

"Oh great Father, no bother at all."

When we saw him that afternoon he was more than delighted to say mass for Ethna's father, looking at his diary, pencilling us in for 7.00 p.m. the following evening. It was an intimate affair, me, Ethna, Fr. Weller, in his office; Ethna sobbed, I tried to look concerned, wishing I was in the pub having a bit of craic.

We did go over to McGowan's afterwards. I ordered two pints of Harp, looking around to see if there were any nice looking fellas.

We joined a group from college including a couple of 4th year guys who stirred my curiosity. The one nicknamed Dokie chatted to me, at one point asking what kind of music I was into; an opportunity to sound interesting offered on a plate. I listed Neil Young, Cat Stevens, James Taylor, saying Roxy Music was my favourite band. The chemistry between us was improving as he watched me drinking my pint with relish; nodding to Ethna that it was time for another.

"Are you a Dylan fan?" he asked.

I reached for my second drink wondering what territory I was heading into.

"Yeh, I really like his early songs, don't really know his latest stuff," no point lying.

"His new film is on in 'The State' tomorrow night, fancy going?

Jesus he was asking me on a date; I hoped he was paying. We decided to meet the following evening, have a few pints before the cinema.

Ethna was chatting to Joey although he seemed to be doing most of the talking while her eyes wandered frequently, watching Dokie and me laughing easily together. She was still quiet on the last bus home so I kept my excitement in check, thinking about Dokie, wondering how we would get on.

He was in McGowan's when I arrived the following evening half way through a pint, his long hair tied back in a ponytail. I hadn't noticed the night before how bad his skin was; as he ordered my drink I knew I didn't fancy him; he was easy company though, so I relaxed, letting the evening take its course.

At 8 o'clock we walked quickly up North Circular Road having stayed too long in the pub. He produced a bag of grass from his coat pocket, unsettling me a little, rolling a huge joint as we hurried along. I hadn't smoked dope before although I craved the experience; this would be another feather in my bohemian cap.

The film had already started and I found it difficult to get my bearings in the dark, packed cinema. We located seats eventually five rows back from the screen amid viewers who whispered aggressively at us to sit down for God's sake.

Bob Dylan was on stage singing about a 'Masterpiece' wearing a strange mask that gave him a ghoulish appearance.

The air around us was rank with the pungent smell of hash, while up on the screen a bunch of people talked in a dark room and I wondered when Joan Baez or Joni Mitchell would start singing.

Dokie lit the joint, sucking heavily on it, passing it to me who mimicked him perfectly, holding the burning smoke in my lungs, exhaling loudly as my head swam, my vision misted. Dylan was now standing in a garage followed by a man who sat on a stage reading a poem, wearing the mask I had seen earlier. My sense of confusion began to mount as the volume grew louder with Dylan on stage backed by five guitars. The sound was big' the song was 'ISIS' and I knew I was seeing things when his face flashed before me covered in flour, white and ghastly.

Pins and needles like electric shocks ran down my arms shooting into my fingers, followed by waves of heat that gripped my body, vice-like, relentless. I struggled to breathe then a terror seized me. I pushed past Dokie, fleeing; telling him I was choking, running through the foyer out into the street. He followed me, confused and shocked as I lunged at passers-by asking them to help me, screaming out that I was having an epileptic fit.

There were puddles on the ground and I ran to them, splashing dirty water on my face to stop the burning in my head while Dokie tried unsuccessfully to calm me down. "I need to go to the hospital!" I shrieked, "I'm dying, I'm dying."

Uncertainty for a moment, then he remembered we were near the Mater. He propelled me along until the Emergency sign came into view and I ran towards it, an oasis in the desert.

I had no sense of decorum, grabbing a young intern, shouting about dying and epileptic fits. Emergency was busy with sprained ankles and broken limbs and I was aware that something dreadful was happening to me with nobody coming to my rescue.

At last two nurses put me in a bed, pulling the curtains around; Dokie unsure whether he should remain by my side as I drew his attention to the cute little creatures who danced on the drapes, smiling and winking at me. Suddenly I knew everyone in the place as I peeped out from my sanctuary, amazed that so many people from home were there.

"Hello Miley, great to see you" waving furiously.

"Hey Frances, what's the craic?" a little hurt that no one replied; maybe they couldn't see me in my cubicle. Eventually the doctor in charge arrived with four young interns in his wake. Shining a light into my eyes I saw the concern as he invited a junior doctor to give his opinion. They whispered about dilated pupils, brain haemorrhage, much to my disappointment.

"No doctor" I said. "My eye has been like that for two years; happened when I was seventeen."

There were relieved faces, particularly that I was making sense, and they discussed my Adie with pleasure and fascination.

"Can you remember exactly how it happened?" an enthusiastic young intern asked me, the others watching, fascinated.

"Oh yeah, I remember well. It was a dark winter's morning, I went into the bathroom and switched on the light and something weird happened to my right eye, my head felt funny too; when I looked in the mirror I noticed one pupil was much bigger than the other and it stayed like that ever since."

"Did you see an ophthalmologist at that time?" another young intern, not bad looking, smiling at me.

"Yeah I did. He put drops in my eye, it was horrible; then he told me not to worry, it was a common enough condition."

I was beginning to enjoy myself. They listened, nodding, focused on the head doctor who warned them about jumping to diagnoses, then turning back to me he wondered if I had taken any form of drug in the cinema. Embarrassed, I told them about the dope, five pairs of eyes blinking, the nice looking one trying not to smile. They left me pulling back the curtain, revealing Dokie sitting in the corridor looking tired, drained. Slowly I began to realise that I wouldn't die as the terrifying symptoms abated. I was given a valium and left to rest for an hour or so.

Dokie insisted on putting me in a taxi; we walked to the rank not a word spoken between us.

It was almost dawn as I walked up the drive to 91. Trying to find my keys, the door opened revealing an eastern looking man I didn't recognise. He gestured, waving to someone as I passed him in the doorway. Rosie was at the bottom of the stairs in a shabby velvet dressing gown. The door slammed; she turned towards me and I smiled, throwing my eyes up to heaven.

"You wouldn't believe the night I had." I needed to tell someone. She produced a crumpled packed of Gold Bond from a velvet pocket and sat on the stairs, lighting her last cigarette, "we'll share it." I sat beside her.

"Well, what the hell happened to ya?"

Like a warrior clutched from the jaws of death I relived the events of the doomed evening, able to laugh then about most of it.

"What did you say the film was called?"

"Renaldo and Clara."

"Well it sounds like a load of shite; sure that old crap would put anyone off the head."

I agreed with her, still unsure whether I imagined the white-faced Dylan. We finished the cigarette and she rose slowly to go.

"I never liked Bob Dylan singing anyway; do you know what he sounds like?" I shook my head. "He's like a young calf roaring in a bucket."

Maeve and Ethna ate their cereal, enthralled as I gave them a blow by blow account of my near death experience.

"I swear girls I thought I was a gonner."

"How did Dokie cope while all this was going on?" misplaced concern on Ethna's part.

"Fuck Dokie, it was his rotten dope that nearly killed me."

"It sounds like a panic attack," Maeve knowledgeable as usual, "we did a paper on that last year."

"Well it felt more like a heart attack," I shook my head woefully.

"No, you'll be grand; research shows that these episodes are best forgotten" Miss Psychologist of the year left the table to get on with her important day.

Ethna and I headed into college where I discovered that infamy preceded me, with older guys nodding knowingly, even administering reassuring pats on my shoulder, confirming that I had been to hell and back.

At lunchtime Dokie spotted me in the canteen surrounded by well wishers, he dropped his gaze, hurrying to the table where his cronies sat, leaving me totally relieved.

Betty who managed the canteen was fast becoming our pal, offering us work washing dishes entitling us to free snacks and lunches. A buxom wench from Roscommon, probably in her early forties, she enjoyed her brandies, singing James Connolly at the drop of a hat. Igniting my rebel tendencies I would join her in the last verse practically roaring 'Oh curse you proud England

32

you cruel-hearted bastards…' before the barman in McGowan's would swoop, warning he would bar us if we kept it up.

We began to notice that McGowan's was being frequented more and more by 'smeara dubha' who were gregarious and pleasant if not a little pushy. Mostly Algerian, the sons of wealthy families sent over to study aircraft engineering at Dublin Airport. They wore designer clothes, flaunting their charms, smelling of expensive colognes while breaking all their strict religious rules. Some of these young men were stunningly beautiful with the odd runt throw in for good measure. In the main though they stood Adonis like, lustrous black curls, chocolate brown eyes and tanned skin. A perfect specimen called Hamid chatted Ethna up on a cold November evening, my pulse quickening wondering where in the crowd his gorgeous friend was lurking.

"Come up, this fella wants to chat to us." Ethna handed me my pint.

"Has he a friend?" smiling as I spoke through clenched teeth.

"Yeah" muttered quickly as she turned towards him, me fast on her heels.

Too late the runt stood, fawning, his beady eyes on me, tongue out slavering.

"How are you pretty lady? My name is Muhammed" he took my hand, kissed it as I demurred, wondering how I could swap, flirt with Hamid instead. There was no exchange as Ethna gazed into those beautiful eyes, me trying to enjoy the barrage of compliments being showered upon me 'til it was time to go home. They invited us to meet them the following evening, promising to take us to a disco near the airport, an offer Ethna felt we couldn't refuse.

8 o'clock, back in McGowan's, the atmosphere was lively with Friday evening revellers at various stages of intoxication, mingling with the newly arrived who were intent on reaching this drunken stage quickly.

Hamid and the runt smiled loudly at our arrival, pointing to saved seats with self-satisfaction. They were suave, attentive, rising quickly to order drinks all evening, lavishing attention with too much intensity. Muhammed was polished, flattering me wildly, becoming more convincing as the night wore on.

"You are a desert flower," kissing my hand again.

"A desert weed you mean," trying to let him down gently.

"Why would I want weeds when I have a rose?" a salacious smile, telling me he wants to take a bite of me.

At one point I looked at my watch and panicked, "Jesus, get up quick, get to the bar and order a few pints, it's closing time, get two each."

Shocked into action the two Lotharios rose quickly giving myself and Ethna time to compare notes.

Those two boys are only after one thing," I gulped down the end of my beer.

"I know, what will we do?"

Two pints were placed before me as I finished my instructions, resuming conversations I looked at my watch again.

"Jesus, it's only half ten, I thought it was half eleven!" laughing, incredulous, realising our dates had time to ply us with a few more drinks.

Closing time loomed, I winked at Ethna as we walked out with our dates, hoping to get a taxi. Standing on the footpath, Hamid watching the traffic, I nudged her and we took to our heels, running down Lower Drumcondra Road, two Olympians, the shock of our departure leaving the boys rooted to the spot. Recovering, they gave chase, our getaway manifesting in the shape of a 16 bus lurching towards the stop on the opposite side of the road. Caught between fear and elation we ran through traffic, diving breathless on to the platform falling on top of each other, laughing like drains, escaping our pursuers who stood in the middle of Dorset Street, open mouthed, defeated.

McGowan's was off limits for a week or two 'til we returned suffering amnesia, blanking the jilted lovers as we took refuge among our college buddies, escaping confrontation.

There were whimpers in college that Christmas tests were being set, giving me palpitations, persuading Ethna to stay late in the library most evenings. Guilt forced me to join her, copying missed lecture notes from generous geeks or trying to source reading material suggested to us in September.

It snowed one evening in mid December as we stood at our infamous stop on Dorset Street, freezing, miserable. Rush hour was long over, we were joined by one other person, a young man who looked Turkish, Moroccan perhaps. He stood opposite us, I thought to myself his features were not beautiful like Hamids. Lost in conjecture I was shocked when Ethna began making faces about him, sticking out her tongue in disgust, scrunching up her nose, smirking at me. I pretended not to notice, aware her target was observant and furious. The bus arrived, we prepared to board, a low guttural noise sounded as something flew through the air hitting the lapel of Ethna's coat. Sliding down the woollen collar a roaming green spittle slithered bringing tears to her eyes, making me recoil, nauseated. We took a seat near the driver afraid to look behind us, terrified the assailant would strike again. There was silence, reaching our stop we jumped off, keys ready fearful until we slammed the door behind us. Ethna was pale and shaken while we prepared supper. I soothed by calling him a crazy fucking bastard, secretly annoyed that she had been so silly, so indiscreet.

Rosie was now a regular visitor and we looked forward to her arrival, listening for the limpedy-limp to our door. Sometimes she wore slippers, making herself comfortable in the pink armchair, now exclusively reserved for her generous posterior. The red polo neck and black skirt never changed despite the cold December winds, neither did the bare, dumpy legs.

She was one of eight children, one sibling living in Dublin, a sister Grainne living in Clondalkin married with three kids.

"Do yas want a tip on how to save a bit of money on the old clothes shopping?" She had the mischievous look again.

We nodded, waiting for her words of wisdom.

"What Grainne does is she swaps the price tags on clothes, so if something is £39.99 she takes a tag saying £9.99 off something else and sticks it on her item, works every time.

"Does she ever get caught?" Ethna was fascinated.

"No, big stores like Dunnes or Penneys have so much stock they haven't a clue at the tills what's what."

We pondered, agreeing that this was brilliant.

She told us she could knit, if any of us wanted a jumper she could finish one in a week. Maeve seized upon this information, "I would love a black polo neck, a really long one, down over my bum." Rosie was amused.

"I'll knit the fucking thing as long as you want it, you supply the wool."

The following evening Maeve arrived with the raw material, a week later Rosie knocked on the flat door, the finished garment in her arms. Pulling it quickly over her head Maeve stood arms askew wondering what we thought.

"Is it long enough?" I asked and we howled.

"It's down to your knees," Ethna snorting.

"Don't listen to them," Rosie snorting too, "it's gorgeous on ya."

"It'll do, I'm wearing it anyway, Maeve sounded determined.

To Rosie's delight the polo neck became Maeve's best friend and she wore it with aplomb as only Maeve could.

A stone-throw from 91 was Garvey's pub, right on Leonard's corner which apparently hosted a talent contest on Friday nights. It was Rosie's weekly indulgence, she invited us to come saying it was craic. We waddled along, the three of us in our jeans and jumpers wrapped up against the cold, behind Rosie in her ubiquitous ensemble, stumpy blue legs leading us to a new watering hole.

The lounge was dingy, dated, with tables on opposite sides of a long, rectangular room. Christmas decorations hung haphazardly, garish tinsel wrapped around fairy lights that flickered randomly from time to time. Sitting near the stage I noticed the customers were mostly old timers, Rosie confirming that Friday was pensioner's night. It was Phantom of the Opera, the organ player grinding out unrecognisable tunes while the old dears sang merrily in thick Dublin accents, volume increasing as the night wore on.

Unbeknownst to me the girls had entered my name as a contestant, they sat complicit, clapping like seals as the competitors took the stage. Some lurched unaided, some oxtered up to sing faltering renditions of 'My Child', 'Catch a Falling Star, pleasing their fans no end.

"A big hand now ladies and gentlemen for Miss Cathy Logue.... Come on up Cathy wherever you are."

"You fucking bitches," all eyes on me.

"Go on, you'll be great," Maeve smirking.

"Ah go on Cathy," Ethna echoing.

"Sure it's only a bit of craic," Rosie encouraging.

Heart racing I approached the grinder hoping I'd remember the words of something. His beady eyes stared through thick spectacles.

"Do you know 'The Night They Drove Old Dixie Down?"

"The night they wha?"

"What about 'You Don't Matter Anymore'?"

"Is that a Sonny Knowles wan?"

"Mary From Dungloe?"

"Ah yeah away ya go, I'll folley ya."

Dreadful accompaniment, I struggled valiantly, watching the girls squirming with delight, the old dears silent, no recognition on their blank faces.

Returning to the table, nonchalant, unwilling to provide further mirth, Rosie soothed.

"Them aul cronies wouldn't know a good song if it bit them on the arse."

Eventually a decrepit old boy won for his rendition of 'Walking the Streets in the Rain' we didn't waste money on more drink, leaving soon after, consoling ourselves with fish and chips on the way home.

'Come up to my place' Rosie ordered, closing the front door.

We were delighted to comply, dying to see what her flat was like. She opened the door to No. 2, a smell met us, damp and mould mixed with something else unsavoury. The cream cooker looked like ours, same sink, same few presses with squalid table and two wooden chairs. It was a tiny space and we huddle round, me sharing a seat with Ethna, eating off the day old newspapers, lighting our Carrols and Gold Bonds, inhaling with pleasure. Her bedroom was up a few more steps on the next landing, we declined the offer to view it, rising to go, wrecked from our week in college.

"Jesus it's a hovel" Ethna pulled the nightdress over her head.

"We thought this place was bad," I sounded sympathetic.

"God love her." Maeve, wise, "We should really let her use our flat when we're not here."

We turned in bed, trying to get comfortable, eventually falling asleep. Sometime in the middle of the night the doorbell rang, waking us, a mistake. I had no intention of answering but they persisted 'til I could stand it no longer, jumping out, furious at the intrusion. A middle aged man, dissipated suit, beard and glasses stood there.

"Rosie Diver?"

"No … No. 2." I pointed upstairs walking back into the flat leaving him to close the front door.

"Who was it?" Maeve's voice full of sleep.

"A horrible looking eejit with a beard, where the fuck is he going this time of night?"

"Maybe it's one of her brothers up from Limerick, stayed late in a nightclub."

"Yeah right, he didn't recognise his own sister."

No reply, she was fast asleep and I thought no more about it, for a while at least.

The following day was Saturday the 16th of December, our last chance to buy Christmas presents before heading home on Wednesday. Ethna and I wept with joy the previous week when the college announced Christmas tests were cancelled due to a number of lecturers being out with flu. Mr. Boyde had vanished mysteriously in late November amid rumours of dismissal. I mourned his absence expecting his replacement to be less enigmatic, less entertaining.

"How much have yous for presents?" the girls were getting dressed.

"I'm not spending a lot, something for mam, that's it," Maeve was an only child, her father died when she was a baby, leaving her with no memory of him except what she could glean from her mother on rare occasions.

"I have about £10" Ethna, flush as usual.

"We'll head down to the Dandelion, hopefully pick up a few things there," second-hand stalls drew me like Aladdin's cave.

The winter sun glared as we walked down Camden Street hoping the day would yield up joy, excitement even romance. The market was heaving with the city's unconventional people trying to look inscrutable, ambling along, clinging to the last vestiges of the hippy era.

A radio blared 'Please Come Home for Christmas' as we walked through the alleyway of boutiques and coffee shops that led to the Dandelion's main courtyard. Familiar smells floated on the air; cigarette smoke, hints of marijuana, the heady scent of patchouli oil mixed with the aroma of freshly brewed coffee. The market was busy, filled with colourful people; girls in vintage fur coats or crocheted capes rifled through bargain boxes and jewellery stalls. Young men stood at record booths, discussing their purchases, Jackson Browne or Steely Dan albums. They smoked, tossing long hair over shoulders, some producing Rizla papers, crafting roll-ups, blowing smoke into the air, exuding contrived untidiness. Rails of second-hand clothes abounded coaxing us, Maeve and I picking through each garment, eager to find the statement piece, the one that quantified our coolness. Ethna hung back, disinterested; unwilling to spend her money on fusty coats or dresses that had been worn by strangers.

A blue fringed poncho, Aztec design, called out to Maeve, I could see it was made truly for her. Declining the offer of a bag she wore the purchase over her flared jeans and mountain boots, a young Cher. I watched her, struggling to keep jealousy at bay. My search among the rails proved fruitless, attention switching to trestle tables that housed classic LP's in mint condition. Mum's present presented itself in the shape of a double Jim Reeves album, a bargain at 80p. A silver tie-pin for 50p sorted Dad out, leaving only my brother Malachy to buy for. He was learning to play drums and my heart soared when a small bodhran caught my eye, perched high up at the back of a stall selling bric a brac. £1.50 stung but my mission was completed. Maeve found her mother's gift there too, a bottle of Bluegrass perfume in a turquoise box, her favourite scent. We browsed aimlessly then, watching the hawkers dealing, striking bargains, holding steaming mugs in fingerless gloves, trying to keep warm. The smell of freshly cooked food wafted, a mixture of sweet and savoury, I realised I was hungry.

"Fancy getting something to eat?" they were both admiring dangly earrings in silver and gold.

"We'll go down to Bewleys," Maeve's suggestion sounded good.

A busker in the alleyway sang 'we've got tonight, who needs tomorrow....' as we walked out past two guys looking angry, fearsome, Mohican hairstyles, safety pins piercing their noses.

"Christ what kind of look is that?" Ethna, shocked.

"Don't know," I shrugged, "hope it doesn't catch on."

The winter sun vanished, walking down Grafton Street promising Ethna we would go to Clerys after lunch. Bewleys was packed with Christmas shoppers, forcing us to share a table with an elderly couple who ate in silence, never once looking at each other. Soup and a roll was the cheapest option and we ate quickly with relish, aware that Ethna's presents were yet to be purchased.

Braving the cold again, a familiar sight appeared outside Switzers, red polo neck, black leather jacket. Rosie holding her clipper-board for a distinguished looking man who wrote on it. Drawing closer we could hear her voice, "Buy a line for autistic children, support autistic children, a worthy cause."

Sneaking up behind her, I shouted "Them aule lines are wild dear!"

"Jesus girls you took the life outta me" she whirled, embarrassed that we saw her working, mystery solved.

"How's business" Ethna strained to get a look at the clipper-board.

"Doing well so far, plenty of people about," she showed us the card, Maeve read the heading.

"In Aid of Autistic Children."

"Does the money go to the whole country or just Dublin?" I was curious.

"I couldn't fucking tell ya," she was adamant, "All I know is I get a tenner for every card sold, with a bit of luck I'll shift three or four of them today."

She looked then as if she wanted us to leave, we were disrupting proceedings. We moved to go, she had a last minute thought.

"The lads in No. 3 had a win on a horse yesterday; there'll be a session later."

We nodded, feigning delight, walking away wondering what 'session' meant.

"I would hate her job." Ethna shook with the cold.

"Could she not at least wear tights?" I sounded angry.

"It's her life," wise Maeve, again.

We stood a moment admiring Clerys' windows decorated beautifully in Dickensian motif, Tiny Tim and Scrooge sat at a table covered in sumptuous food, an array of toy, gifts strewn at their feet.

The store thronged, Ethna led the way, determined gait pushing to the rear, taking wide stairs to the first floor. My boredom was thinly disguised, searching among tailored coats, dresses, sensible blouses and cardigans, expensive price tags. Undeterred, Ethna persisted, achieving her goal, two blouses, two shirts later, mother, sister, brothers, job done.

"It's easy when ya have money," she ignored me, we wandered into the hat emporium. Maeve loved to wear berets, French style, suited her perfectly. Ethna treated herself to a wide-brimmed black hat, maroon sash, weeks previously, it gave her a rakish appearance worn over the long yellow tresses. My turn now. Surely there was a hat to give me kudos, make my mousy short hair remarkable, scream 'CATHY LOGUE, DEEP, BEAUTIFUL, ETHEREAL.'

Placing a tan affair, cowboy style on my head, Maeve was animated.

"That is gorgeous on you."

The mirror screamed 'CATHY LOGUE, DEEP, BEAUTIFUL, ETHEREAL', what price was it, fumbling to see the tag. Right, there was only one thing to do. Hat on, as in a dream, I moved slowly, calmly, through the fashion floor, stopping to admire a jacket here, a dress there, going towards the stairs, unwilling accomplices behind me, hearts beating like drums. Floating down the stairs, causal, relaxed, stopping for a spray of Charley, heavy front doors just inches away.

Through the doors, onto O'Connell Street, temples pulsating, palms soaked, silence 'til we crossed the bridge into Westmorland Street.

I gazed over my shoulder, "Think I got away with it girls."

Ethna, silent, her closed face impossible to read.

Maeve, pragmatic. "You managed it this time but don't bloody well try that again."

Relief infected, filled us up, we laughed throwing our heads back, me holding tight to my new accessory, delighted, successful.

Returning to Grafton Street on our way to the Indian shop we waved at Rosie, still nabbing charitable shoppers. Maeve wanted patchouli oil, while she sniffed bottles Ethna tired on a colourful dress. My accomplished larceny gave further courage. A red coat beckoned, ethnic crossover design in roughly hewn fabric, inciting greed. Rosie's advice echoed, hands moved deftly switching tags, I approached the counter.

"How much is this?" holding out the coat.

Slender brown hands rummaged through fabric, "Ah here it is…. £8," no suspicion in her eyes.

"Can I write a cheque, I have a banker's card?" There'd be some explaining to do when Mum got the bank statement.

I relaxed then, sated, magnanimous, encouraging Ethna to buy the dress, Maeve the perfume, not a trace of envy haunting my mind.

We walked through the dusky streets, smog descending the closer we got to 91, making us long for the warmth of a big turf fire.

We allowed ourselves the luxury of the two-bar heater after our day's shopping, aware the meter ate up 50p pieces. In the bedroom clothes flew, strewn, the genesis of Christmas packing, rucksacks pulled from under beds, compliments swapped, outfits decided. We borrowed, traded, I mostly borrowed, Ethna kindly handing over shirts and shoes she probably wouldn't wear over the holidays. Maeve rustled up scrambled eggs and toast, putting on one of the two LPs we owned, hogging the heater, Rod Stewart's voice rising 'First Cut is the Deepest.' Noises in the hall, knock on our door, I rose to answer it.

A motley crew greeted me; Pat and Dominic from No. 3 smiling, swaying slightly, introducing their friend Carina who slurred "Howya?" revealing prominent teeth, dull vacant eyes giving her a goofy look. Rosie took up the rear, limpedy-limping in behind the others, easing herself into her pink throne. Ethna and Maeve pulled out chairs amid jovial "How are yas?" and "Sit downs" spotting the brown paper bags under oxters, full of alcohol. We had nicknamed the lads 'Little 'n' Large';

Pat, long and lanky, dark hair receding above a flat non-descript face; Dominic, a petite hamster, little beady eyes, tiny hands and feet.

"Now there's plenty of booze girls," Pat announced, brown bags placed on the table. "Get some glasses and help yourselves."

Four cups, three tumblers and an opener were produced, Dominic doing barman, handing out bottles of beer, vodka and cokes. The atmosphere was warm, amiable, as we drank, chatted, laughed; Rosie delighted she had sold four cards, the men recounting the final moments of the race where their horse was victorious.

"How did the shopping go women?" Rosie accepting her second beer.

"Went really well, didn't it Cathy?" Ethna sneering.

"Will I show ya what I got?" jumping up before she could answer, going into the bedroom; I emerged donning my new hat and coat. Wolf whistles, Rosie's eyes bulged with curiosity.

"Jaysus, you were fairly spending today," her eyebrows raised.

"Oh Cathy can find the bargains." Maeve winked.

I twirled, "Put it like this, your advice came in handy" more winking, giggling, watched by the lads who giggled too, a far away look in their eyes, still watching their horse romping home a winner.

"Give us another volka there" Carina slurred through buck teeth, unleashing more laughter, nudging, winking; Rod singing 'Tonight's the night…. It's gonna be alright…'

Without warning the meter snapped, Rod stopped singing, the two red bars faded to black. We had one 50p left in the kitty which returned creature comforts, though we were on borrowed time. Worried brows were calmed by our unlikely heroes, now well inebriated they came to the rescue.

"Give us a knife someone and I'll show ye a little trick" Dominic bounded delicately towards the meter; an educational demonstration ensued, skilled movements of the knife, the meter now full, enough electricity to last a week. Ecstasy; the three of us practiced, Dominic praising, our apprenticeship completed.

Pat was not to be outdone "Put off the feckin heater and we'll light a decent fire in dat lovely grate," he disappeared into the hall reappearing weighed down with phone books, tripping towards the marble fireplace. Minutes later the chimney roared, we pulled chairs, sofa closer, watching flames dancing as years of phone numbers went up in smoke. Hearts warmed, we sang, chatted, sang some more, clinking our glasses; Carina calling for more volka 'til drink ran out and we burned all but the current directory, leaving a strip of dust free linoleum in the hall.

They left amid 'Goodnights', 'Happy Christmas' we returned to the dying embers, lighting nightcap cigarettes; analysing, rehashing, mimicking. Traffic died down, we turned in our beds knowing sleep would come quickly.

"Will we hitch home on Wednesday Maeve, save the bus fare?"

"Aye, good idea. Can't wait for Christmas now."

The sentiment floated in the air; I sank heavy hearted knowing it would be a nightmare.

Wednesday morning Ethna headed to Heuston Station, Norma, her older sister was picking her up in Cork City to bring her home; fresh out of college she had landed a job teaching in the local national school.

Maeve and I made a cardboard sign the night before saying 'DONEGAL' carrying it on the bus to Finglas where we'd begin our journey home. We wrapped up well, Maeve in her black polo neck and jeans under the blue poncho, black beret pulled sideways over her left ear. I couldn't resist wearing my new hat and coat over an Aran cardigan and jeans, aware that the inquisition would begin as soon as mum saw me. Being out fairly early paid off, standing on the roadside in Finglas holding up our sign, we watched as more and more lined up in front of us sticking out their thumbs hoping to be lifted despite the fact that we were first in line. Our breaths came out smoky in the frosty air, we chatted, putting our rucksacks on the cold ground, having to lift them quickly again running to the blue BMW pulling in beside us, the driver shouting through the passenger window.

"I'm only going as far as Monaghan if that's any good to you?"

"Yeah, that's fantastic" delighted when I saw how handsome he was.

Maeve opened the front door dragging her rucksack awkwardly in with her, relegating me to the back seat. After a while I didn't mind this arrangement, he fancied himself an intellectual, pontificating to Maeve who was delighted to display her brilliance. He remembered to look in the rear view mirror at me now and again but he was totally taken with Maeve, looking at her too often for comfort, instead of watching the road, going ninety miles an hour; typical. Sitting in a tailback in Carrigmacross the one o'clock news came on, making me uneasy, igniting debate in the front.

"Those guys in Long Kesh have a lot to answer for," he shifted into second gear as traffic moved.

"What do you mean?" Maeve's voice challenged.

"They're the cause of this terrible violence in Londenderry and Belfast right now."

"Those men are political prisioners, they're being treated like animals by the British government.

"Oh come on now, you don't truly believe that, do you?" clipped northern accent.

I let them at it, silently agreeing with everything Maeve said, knowing he was smug, a million miles removed from the reality of the situation.

Pleasantries had resumed by the time we reached Monaghan, waving goodbye, shivering in the biting wind, the town clock tolled twice and our stomachs rumbled with hunger. A prefabricated café in the square was our usual haunt when we came that way, serving decent food at a reasonable price. We sat, rucksacks on the floor, delighted when Maeve found two stray fifty pences in her bag, meaning we could order tea, bread and butter with our sausage, beans and chips. I left my hat on the chair beside me promising I wouldn't forget it.

"You were right to tell that posh fucker what you thought."

"Hmmmm, don't know, I think he was just flirting with me."

"You reckon?" I wasn't going to encourage a big head.

"God it's nearly three o'clock, we better get back out there, it'll be dark soon," she swallowed down her last drop of tea pointing at my hat.

"Hope we get a lift through the North" my voice anxious, aware of dangers lurking in war torn territory.

A light dusting of snowflakes descended, we stood near the Four Seasons Hotel displaying our sign, longing to be home. A heavy articulated lorry flashed its lights, we ran once again struggling to get into the high elevated seat beside the driver, holding tight to my hat. Initially the view from the truck was thrilling but spirits flagged when he announced he was stopping in Omagh for the night.

"You're welcome ladies to stay with me" sexy French accent, he pointed to the bunk behind him.

We laughed, preferring to brave the cold Northern highway to his seedy invitation.

We left him at a lay-by on the edge of town, walking through Omagh, daylight fading. Snow was falling heavier, there was little conversation, holding up our sign, thumbs out, hearts beating too loudly with every armoured car that passed.

Then up on the road it came. Speeding by us, a screech of breaks, backing up, sleek silver Cortina. Three young men late twenties looked out at us, very short hair, inexplicably I though 'shit, student priests!' moving towards the car. Maeve, more alert muttered sideways 'Oh fuck!', too late, I opened the door to hell.

Still unenlightened, pushing in beside the back seat passenger, Maeve after me, rucksacks balancing awkwardly on our knees; door barely closed the car accelerated, stones flew, the driver spoke turning his head to look at us.

"All right girls?" heavy English accent, green eyes fixed on us, not the road.

"Fine thanks," Maeve sounded nervous.

They laughed, too loudly, unpleasantly, reality began to dawn.

"Guess where we've just been girls?" driver looking over his shoulder again, the smell of alcohol reaching my nose.

"At a wedding?" trying to keep my voice steady.

More forced provocative laughter, three sets of eyes staring, car speeding along on auto pilot, snowflakes hitting the windscreen.

"No, not a fucking wedding, was it guys? Tell them where we've been Andy."

"We've just been to the funeral of our mate, shot dead by a scummy IRA bastard" the voice beside me, warm in my ear.

My stomach heaved and my heart began racing, something rolled touching my shoe, a hand grenade; now I knew.

I knew we were going to die; these three plain-clothed British soldiers, drunk and angry, would drive up a side road when they tired of us; news headlines rang in my head 'RAPED AND MURDERED ----- TWO YOUNG DONEGAL GIRLS FOUND.'

"You ever see a real gun girls?" the front passenger looked around, pointing a pistol.

We didn't answer, watching his sneering mouth; trapped. I remembered the battered faces of the men in Long Kesh who looked out at us from the poster in the local Sinn Fein shop, how angry it made us, Maeve and I agreeing to sell An Phoblacht to the girls in boarding school. His brummie accent jarred, I wanted to shout

The back seat embraced us, warmth seeped into our bones, we melted into the upholstery, glad they were a quiet couple. Boney M sang "Hark now hear the angels sing a king is born today" cruising towards home I looked at Maeve in her black beret; gasping "my hat, my fucking hat!" whispering loudly. Her eyes popped and she made an O shape with her mouth, then stifled a giggle with her hand. I threw my eyes to heaven; oh well, easy come easy go, the vision of a half cocked British soldier driving along in a lady's hat swam before my eyes.

The Logue Christmas was unhappy. Dad used it as an excuse to go on a bigger bender than usual, arriving late to midnight mass, shouting obscenities at the back of the chapel. We opened presents Christmas morning, faking happiness, ignoring the disparaging grunt from him as he threw his tie-pin back under the tree. Malachy and I frequented the disco, taking refuge in drink ourselves, unable to truly enjoy, carrying unhappiness around like heavy loads. Oddly mum compensated, giving me money on New Year's Eve to buy a new outfit, a gesture I accepted gleefully. She liked my new coat, delighted that I got it on a sale rack for only £4. I'd worry about the cheque later. The last night of 1978, Maeve appeared in the pub, four interesting looking fellas in tow; I felt the load easing gently as they ambled towards me, confident in my new jeans and suede cowboy boots.

"This is the guys from Rustic," she introduced them one by one, spoiled for choice, who would I make a play for?

Finian had the looks that appealed, a head of dark spiral curls, piercing green eyes, sallow complexion. He wore a black waistcoat over a pale blue grandfather shirt, torn jeans and boots, dashing, Gallic.Liam, Dan and Olly more typically Irish, though not unattractive wore their faded jeans, their baggy jumpers with a little less elegance, a little less style. They were laid back company, open and friendly, conversing easily, my attention focused mainly on Finian.

"So what do you play?" I held his gaze.

"Uilleann pipes mostly, guitar too."

"Have you never heard them Cathy?" Maeve sounded incredulous.

"No, but I'd love to."

"Oh, they're fantastic. That was a great gig in The Fiesta last week Finian," her brown eyes smouldered, I realized she was flirting with him.

"Game on," I thought, moving closer, touching his arm as I spoke, aware that my thigh brushed his, delicious little shocks rippling through me.

Disadvantaged, Maeve sat opposite, conceding defeat when the bells rang in the New Year and he kissed me on the mouth, taking my breath away; she switched her attention to Liam who sat in the wings waiting.

Being from Derry I knew Finian had a long drive home, still I didn't ask him in when he stopped at my door, the kitchen light a beacon, warning of dangers within.

"We'll be up in Dublin in two week's time" his arm behind me on the headrest.

"Maeve said we could stay in your flat."

"God yous are welcome," wishing he would kiss me again.

"Right we'll see you then" he moved towards me, our mouths met, he tasted of tobacco and beer his breath warm, sweet.

"Yeah, see you then," getting out of the car, smiling, waving as he drove away; I turned sighing heavily, the noise of raised voices reaching my ears.

Malachy was in before me, a chink of light visible under his bedroom door. Despite the drunk ranting downstairs I fell asleep, hugging myself, imagining sallow muscular arms around me, savouring the fluttering joy of anticipation.

Maeve rang on Wednesday; Dad answered.

"It's that McLaughlin tramp on the phone."

"Hi Maeve, what's the craic?"

"How did you get on last night?"

"Great. He's fucking gorgeous; they're coming up to us in two week's time. Did you go with Liam?"

"No. He walked me home, came in for a cup of tea and we just chatted."

"Oh. I thought he was really nice."

"Aye he's grand, not exactly my type" a slight threat in her voice?

"Right. Are you heading back on Sunday?"

"Yeah, Mum said she'll drop us to the bus, we'll pick you up at half four."

I was content to spend the last few days watching 'Doctor Zhivago' 'Gold Finger', whatever films R.T.E. showed, joined by Malachy who made doorstep sandwiches after Mum went to bed and we had the sitting room to ourselves. As soon as Dad's car pulled up we slunk off to bed, listening to his diatribe, pretending to be asleep. Malachy yearned for Sunday too, dying to return to Killybegs where he was training to be a chef; his course finished in May, then he would never live at home again.

Sunday kindly arrived; I packed my rucksack after late mass, leaving it in the hall, watching anxiously for Maeve's blue Escort estate, hiding my joy as Mum scolded about overspending while Dad held his head in his hands emitting low mournful gasps.

It felt good to be back in 91, no nagging, no violent outbursts, no foreboding. Ethna returned laden down with meat and vegetables from the farm providing us with decent food for a week, a welcome change from beans or scrambled eggs on toast. Monday morning on the 16 bus I told her about our drama with the British soldiers, urging her to keep it to herself. I told her about Finian too though she seemed unimpressed by either topic.

"So what kind of time had you?"

"Grand out. Went to the pub in Schull a few evenings. Went up to Cork with Norma one of the days, she wanted to get crayons and plasticine for her class."

"Is there a disco near you?" so far it sounded boring.

"There's the odd dance in Skib but I couldn't be bothered going."

"Any talent about?"

"Not really, a lot of lads have emigrated to England or America," her voice matter of fact.

"Christ," I thought, "that place sounds like a barrel of laughs."

Upstairs in room 1 Mr. Brennan, our new English lecturer walked confidently through the door carrying a heavy briefcase. A tall bulk, in his forties I surmised, navy sports jacket, pressed grey slacks. He was strangely attractive though his features were irregular; a jutting jaw-line, crooked nose, black square glasses; a bespectacled grizzly bear. He quickly commanded with his booming voice making it obvious that he was brilliant, on top of his subject. Memories of Mr. Boyde faded as I listened to this commanding man. We would be reading Tess of The D'Urbervilles, the Romantic poets, Hamlet; I made my way quickly to the lost property cubbyhole under the stairs hoping to find a copy of at least one text there.

Fr. Magee in Education outlined a project we had to undertake; it involved interviewing the family of a special needs child to discover the effects that had on their world or interviewing a person who turned their life around in some way; we could present it on tape or in writing. I liked the second option, knew exactly what I'd do.

Micro-teaching was beginning Monday morning the 15th when 6th class pupils from Eccles St. Primary School would come into the studio downstairs; we would film and be filmed in pairs as we taught a ten minute lesson to these amused, eager young girls. Lectures no longer finished at lunchtime; the honeymoon was over, no more rushing out to meet in each other's flats, smoking, listening to music or mooching about town practising my light-fingered skills.

Maeve was staying in college 'til all hours, aiming for 1.1 in her degree amid rumours that the top three in the class would secure a bursary to Berkley University to do a masters.

Rosie was still limedy-limping in the hall with her clipper-board, stopping for chats, waiting for her taxi, destination Grafton Street. Doorbell activity increased, peaking after closing time, a dull resignation settled as Ethna, Maeve or myself lurched sleepwalking to the front door in our brush cotton nighties, pointing towards No. 2, hearing the same inquiry "Rosie Diver?" On occasion Rosie's head would appear over the banister, her eyes vetting these nocturnal guests, all smelling of alcohol, all remarkable in their ugliness.

For a while I had been aware of strange, unpleasant sensations running through my body, struggling to ignore the pins and needles in my fingers, the tightening in my throat, little echoes of my nightmare in the cinema. Hangovers became acute, smoking no longer a pleasure, worrying me into considering giving up cigarettes and alcohol completely. Loneliness sat on my shoulders making me clingy, following Ethna around, shadowing Maeve, no longer secure in my own company.

On Saturday Ethna wanted to visit her cousin in Blackrock, I tagged along, reluctant to stay in the flat alone as Maeve was spending the day at a friend's flat working on assignments. We sat upstairs on the crowded No. 7, Ethna proffered the cigarette packet which I declined watching a dark haired young man rising at the front of the bus ringing the bell for the next stop. Without warning a current of heat like a wave of electricity swept through me, pins and needles surged, invisible hands about my throat, choking, choking.

"I have to get off, get up, let me off."

Pushing out of the seat we followed the young man down the stairs out into the air, gasping, distraught, Ethna's bewildered eyes watching me, helpless. A church lay just ahead, I ran towards it hoping that inside lay salvation, peace. Kneeling down weeping, praying "Dear wee God make this go away, please dear Jesus." Wringing hands pleading; I heard Ethna's voice, calm, reasonable.

"St. Vincent's is only across the road, come on, we'll go over."

Vague hope descended and I trotted behind her, invisible band now tightening around my head, struggling to swallow my saliva. Emergency was quiet, a nurse attended immediately, a young doctor shone his little torch down my throat finding no obstruction, no signs of abnormality. Of course my one dilated pupil fascinated, I explained wearily its origin sad that no physical illness was discovered. Still my symptoms abated, we walked out into the fresh January day, deflated. Unable to face another bus journey I asked Ethna to walk back to 91 with me, she could visit her cousin another day.

Maeve returned at 6 o'clock, shocked by my tormented eyes, she listened, comforted.

"I think it's called a flashback."

"What does that mean?" I was crying.

"It means the weird feelings you got the time you smoked grass in the cinema can come back days, weeks, even months later, torture you all over again.

"Jesus, will they last long?" hope evaporating.

"I don't know. Maybe we should go out tonight, have a few drinks take your mind off it."

"No, I couldn't, I think I'll go to bed."

The night was harrowing, endless, struggling to sleep, listening to the girls chatting, laughing easily in the next room, begging God to free me from this misery. Back in college Monday morning I asked to see Fr. Weller who listened while I described my symptoms, omitting the dope smoking incident. He made an appointment with his own physician, driving me to the surgery door. Frustration continued as he could find nothing physically wrong either. Realisation dawned; I would have to battle on silently, eventually I would wake up from this bad dream.

Tuesday morning, the bus turned on to Dorset Street, a poster in "The Meeting Place," window announced 'RUSTIC' Traditional Band Saturday 7pm, Admission 50p.

"Jesus, I nearly forgot," I pointed it out to Ethna. "They're staying with us you know."

"What do you call the lad you like?"

"Finian, he's gorgeous, they're all nice, you might fancy Dan or Olly."

"You never know," her voice bland.

We spent the next few days getting a lesson plan together for the micro-teaching Monday morning, settling on Forgiveness as our theme for the ten minute stint. I concocted a story about a man who fell out with his daughter, after he died she found a note addressed to her telling her he was heartbroken they never reconciled. I would tell the pupils this story then Ethna would read The Prodigal Son followed by questions, brainstorming which scenario was the most positive, most healing.

"Thank God that's done," Ethna sounded relieved.

"Yeah, we can enjoy the weekend now. Let's go home, plan what we'll wear, I might borrow your green cords."

"I was going to wear them myself but you can borrow something else."

"Sure I'll have a look," delighted to have access to her wardrobe.

We put 50p in the meter keeping Tommy Heenan happy, experts now with the knife, he never mentioned the missing phone books.

We left college early Friday giving ourselves time to tidy the flat, allowing me to perfect my look, trying to echo Finian's offbeat artistic style. Maeve got in around four looking effortlessly unorthodox in her mauve Indian kaftan worn over faded flares. I tucked Ethna's khaki grandfather shirt into my Neil Young jeans displaying their backside embroidered in a patchwork of vintage materials painstakingly copied from the sleeve of After the Goldrush. The suede cowboy boots were my 'je ne se quois' giving me confidence, quelling butterfly wings flapping too strongly in my tummy. Ethna wore her green cords with distinctive masculine braces over a floral cotton shirt achieving an image I envied, a coolness she was oblivious to. I wished my hair was longer, blonder, as Rod sang, the two-bar heater glowed, the mirror above the empty grate reflected back my anxious face applying a last layer of lip gloss; the doorbell rang.

"Well hello there," Maeve's voice in the hall.

They trouped in behind her, a fanfare of denim, long hair, curls, nodding heads, smiles, carrier bags filled with beers, chocolate, crisps, placed on the sitting room table. Rod sang 'You keep me hanging on'; Ethna and I sat cross legged on the pink sofa, exhaling cigarette smoke, striking a balance between laid back and friendly. Their easy, relaxed company filled the room with a banter that ebbed, flowed gently, comfortably.

Finian sat in Rosie's throne, the most talkative, gesticulating, even at times acting out his anecdotes vaudeville style, making us laugh hysterically. We opened beers becoming more animated as the evening passed, encouraging the boys to bring in their instruments from the van outside, which they did, along with sleeping bags that had visited many flats it seemed. Liam's guitar playing was hypnotic, he breathed heavily, plucking strings, a self composed air called the Heather Glen floated, we swayed gently watching his fingers working magic.

"Cathy for a song," Maeve winked.

"Go on Logue," Ethna was beginning to slur.

The boys made encouraging noises, the beers gave me confidence.

"OK, I'll try Down by the Sally Gardens."

"Oh lovely, what key?" Finian's guitar was poised.

Seeing uncertainty in my eyes Olly helped "Just start, we'll follow you."

I heard my voice, sweet gentle vibrato, guitars picking up the tune, dulcet mandolin strings from Dan, Olly on tin whistle, crescendo.

"That's was pretty good" Finian seemed surprised.

Triumph faded as I watched Liam rolling a joint, feeling trapped, knowing it was perfectly acceptable with the others. The pungent smell rose inviting invisible hands that fluttered round my neck, pins and needles stabbing. I rose, excusing myself, I needed the loo. Using all my wiles I avoided refusing a toke, relieved when the munchies set in, we tore open crisp bags, sucked on chocolate, sticking out tongues displaying brown molten blobs making us cry with laughter. Somehow Finian had found his place beside me, holding my hand; bedtime beckoned. Liam, Dan, Olly unrolled their sleeping bags, no expectations of joining Maeve or Ethna in the bedroom. Giving the girls time to get undressed I led Finian inside, stripping to our underwear we snuggled under the covers waiting for slow rhythmic breathing telling us the girls were asleep. Again his kiss was sensuous, tender, awakening urges I would not give into in a flat with five other people. Finian implored with expert touches, eventually turning his back, falling into a deep frustrated sleep. It was late Saturday morning, we awoke, glad when Finian left the room, we dressed quickly hearing kitchen presses opening and closing, disappointing the boys with bare shelves. Maeve was the first to join them, apologising for the lack of food, giving Ethna and I a chance to talk.

"How did you get on?"

"I'd say he expected you know what but he didn't get it."

"Too bad about him."

"I know but it'll be really awkward now I suppose."

Maeve put her head around the bedroom door. "Finian and I are driving up to the shop to get stuff for a fry up, won't be long. The front door slammed, I watched them behind the dusty netted curtain in the bay window, laughing, driving off, a weariness descending as my temples throbbed, my heart sank.

At 5 o'clock we piled into the van, sitting on the floor among speakers, microphones, miles of flex, heading to The Meeting Place. The lads would set up the equipment well in advance, then we could relax, enjoy the pints they would buy us with money they had made from their last gig in Derry. We helped, carrying the gear; a cross between roadies and groupies, thrilled to be with the band, escaping the cover charge, anticipation rising as the doors opened and the upstairs lounge packed quickly. A young woman from Clare accompanied by a guitar player stood on the stage, the support act, looking a year or two older than myself. She opened with a song by Pumpkinhead, the hairs stood on the back of my neck; "When I find out that you don't love me baby...." Christ her voice was amazing, she didn't need a mic, her strong deep folky tones filled the room. Three songs later she finished her set, my head reeled knowing I could never sing like that, gulping my pint of Harp as 'Rustic' took to the stage.

Finian was a natural front man, introducing the band, announcing the names of each set of reels, hornpipes, singing old Irish ballads himself, the audience responded, clapping in time to the tunes, cheering loudly, shouting for more at the end of the session. Olly had given us money earlier, instructing us to keep the pints coming while they played, an order Ethna took to heart, staggering to the stage too frequently, depositing pints in front of a confused Dan, in an awkward gesture of courtship.

It was almost midnight when we parked the van around the corner and walked up South Circular to 91. Rosie was in the hall finishing a phone call, she eyed the carryout bags Dan and Olly held, wearing her usual outfit, feet sandwiched into blue furry slippers.

"Yes ladies, how's it going?" she glanced at the lads surreptitiously.

"Grand" the others had walked past her into the flat. I felt the need to explain.

"Who's the weirdos?" she nodded towards the flat.

"They're in a band called 'Rustic', just played The Meeting Place. Sure come on in and meet them."

She turned quickly, limpedy limping in before me. I watched her behind waddle thinking her arse was getting bigger by the day.

"Hi Curly, that's my fucking seat" making a beeline for the pink armchair, Finian jumped up, smirking though his eyes blazed.

"Everyone for a beer?" Dan had begun opening bottles.

"Jesus I'd love one, I'm parched," Rosie tried unsuccessfully to cross her dumpy legs.

Olly's bemused face handing her the bottle of Smithwicks mirrored the faces of Liam and Dan while Finian, demoted to the arm of the sofa, watched her as one would a strange species of human just recently discovered. The two red bars glowed yet the room was cold. Rosie's bare legs made me shiver.

"Have you anything to light a fire with girls?" Liam must have felt it too.

"They have fuck all, they burned all the fodder there was about the place before Christmas."

The memory of the charred phone books made us snigger, confusing the lads further, Rosie's belly spasmodic, snorting uncontrollably, the beer bottle jumping in her hand.

Finian became determined, moving the circular table sideways he stood, staring at a dilapidated chest of drawers that had remained empty and unused.

"Give us a hand here boys, this looks like fire material to me." It broke like tinder under heavy mountain boots, placed around crumpled brown bags and set alight we cheered as it crackled and sparked in the grate.

"Tommy Heenan'll go off his fat fucking head," brown eyes danced in Rosie's face.

"Fuck Tommy Heenan," Ethna slurred, placing her hand on Dan's knee causing him to look confused, though she seemed not to notice.

Another drawer was dismantled, added to the fire as more beers were opened, a welcome heat spreading through the room creating a red pattern on Rosie's naked legs. She produced a packed of ten Gold Bond, offering them to shaking heads who produced their own Carrols, Majors, while Liam once again rolled a joint, lighting up, inhaling deeply, passing it to Rosie who sat next to him.

She took it, returning her unlit cigarette to the box, smoking in the same manner she would a darling Gold Bond. She held court, puffing away on the reefer, flicking the ash on the hearth, telling us about her day outside Switzers.

"The fucking Guards had me tortured," she took another drag of the joint, this time looking at it distastefully.

"Do you not have a permit?" Detective Maeve on the job.

"I do, but they hound me, asking stupid auld questions, bloody gobshites. A jumped up fucker today wanted to know if I was the person who refused to pay a taxi man who left me at the bottom of Grafton Street. Says

I 'I have no idea what you are on about' you want to see the way he was looking at me. I fecked off early when I saw Brennan's head down at Trinity around 5 o'clock."

"Brennan?" Ethna was trying hard to concentrate.

"Sergeant Brennan, a Kerry eejit."

The boys were watching the reefer hungrily, I encouraged her, urged on by the contempt that lingered in Finian's fierce green eyes.

"God Rosie, how did you recognise him that far away?"

"Ah I would know his auld arse if it was sticking out through a hole in the ditch."

I howled, Ethna struggled to keep her eyes open. Finian's face was etched in disgust. She rose to go, taking a last drag of the reefer then flicking it into the dying fire.

"I don't' know what brand of cigarettes you boys smoke but that fag tasted like shite."

Limpedy-limp out she went, pulling the door behind her, shuffling up the stairs to the hovel she called home.

Finian was scathing; "The ignorant heap, bloody culchie, did you see what she did with the joint? She's probably a Big Tom fan." He looked at Maeve, she returned his gaze with a little too much intensity, her mouth pouted.

"Actually she is a Big Tom fan, so what?" I sounded angry.

"Oh come on Cathy," superior Maeve emerging.

There was a buzzing in my ears and the invisible band around my head began to tighten. Ethna was snoring, slumped up against Dan, the left side of her face pulled down grotesquely. Dan's own head was nodding, as was Liam's while the last drawer from the sideboard petered out in the grate.

"Come on Ethna, time for bed," I helped her inside, keeping my back towards the others, ignoring Maeve's 'goodnight' blessing, banging the bedroom door behind me.

I awoke Sunday morning expecting to find Finian in Maeve's bed but he wasn't there, taking the edge off my indignation. Ethna was still snoring, aware that the cupboards were bare I turned and fell asleep again 'til the noise of a key tapping the bedroom door woke me around 12 o'clock.

"Girls we're going to head now," it was Finian's voice. Maeve was up like a shot, pulling on her silky dressing gown, shoving her feet into cosy mules, she exited the room. Low muttering, then Olly's voice audible, "Thanks a million for the hospitality, see you when yous are down again."

"No bother, see ya lads, see ya Finian," no doubt she was giving him the little pout, the killer look.

Too many beers the night before exacerbated the tightness in my throat, the feeling of dread that hung around me. There was relief when Maeve dressed quickly, announcing her departure to her friend Mary's flat to finalise work on college assignments, she would bring back something for evening tea.

"Logue have you any money?" Ethna's voice still under the blankets.

"No, not a penny, I'll change a cheque tomorrow. Have you any?"

"I have enough for bread and fags."

"At least we can have toast, I'm going to try and give us smoking, see does it help these horrible symptoms of mine."

"Right, I'll get up in a minute and go round to the shop."

We spent the afternoon practising for micro-teaching, reading our stories to a pretend audience, working on the questions we would ask the young girls on Monday morning.

6.30pm Maeve arrived back with egg rolls and chips from the Chinese in Rathmines which we reheated under the grill, eating with relish, Rod in the background singing 'Hot Legs' making me choke with giggles.

"What the hell are you laughing at?" Maeve smiling, glad I was thawing out.

"That song's reminding me of Rosie's wee stumps in front of the fire last night."

Ethna blushed, remaining silent, focusing intently on the contents of her egg roll.

"Jesus, she's some detail, she doesn't give a fuck." I laughed again.

"Now the boys weren't too impressed with her" no hint of malice in Maeve's voice.

Aware that she had generously bought our tea with her grant money made me magnanimous. "The poor fellas, bet they never saw the likes of her before."

We concentrated on Rosie for a while, careful not to mention Dan or Finian or Liam or Olly.

"Did ye notice the size of Rosie's backside?" Ethna found her voice.

"I know, she has an arse on her now the size of Limerick." Maeve rubbed her hands in her usual gleeful way. "She could hardly fit on her throne."

"It might be a good thing" I sounded mysterious.

"Why?" Maeve and Ethna in unison.

"With a big of luck she'll burst out of that bloody jumper and skirt. Wouldn't it be amazing to see her in a new outfit!"

Ethna and I were scared stiff in college Monday morning, rehashing every word we intended saying until our turn came and we stood before the Eccles St. girls. Ten minutes felt like an hour, although they responded well, answering our questions, smiling conspiratorially as if paid to make us look good. The following evening Mr Grogan replayed our strengths and weaknesses on a television in room 4. I hated how my voice sounded, the drawly northern accent, silently promising to neutralise it the next time. Both of us looked a stone heavier on screen, playing havoc with my fragile self-image while Ethna seemed immune to any of the feedback, positive or negative.

In Education, Fr. McGee reminded us we had a week to produce our project work, to be read out or played for the entire class. Ethna's cousin in Blackrock had a neighbour with a Down's Syndrome child, she was more than happy to do an interview as long as Ethna showed her the questions. I wanted to interview an ex-drug addict, an English guy who drank in Slattery's of Rathmines who had an eye on Maeve; I hoped she would set it up for me. He was a lot older, attractive in a rakish kind of way, long hair, unusual goatee beard growing in two separate tufts jutting half a foot from his chin.

"Do you know where he lives, Maeve?" we were sitting at the heater.

"Yeah I was in his flat a few times, I don't know about just arriving at his door though."

"I'm sure he won't mind, if we go up Saturday afternoon, I'll have the tape recorder with me, we'll see how it goes."

Friday evening Pat and Dominic dropped in, Rosie in tow, the lads kind, handing out beers liberally, surprised at my refusal to join in the smoking or drinking; Rosie glancing at me from time to time, her eyes oscillating between concern and intrigue. Tommy Heenan had been around earlier collecting rent, emptying the metre, seemingly happy enough with the three 50p's he found there, oblivious to the missing drawers.

"We're a dab hand with the knife now, Dominic." I tried sounding jovial.

"And Heenan never notices, wha?" He seemed delighted.

"Give him as little as yous can girls" Pat, paternal, "for he's the meanest so and so God put on the planet, see the state of these flats and the bathroom."

"Bathroom," Rosie, warming to the topic, "there's cows eating outa nicer baths in the fields around Limerick."

The conversation continued in that vein for a while, by the time they left Tommy Heenan's ears may have been on fire.

Standing at the open door Rosie asked us again if we fancied selling lines some weekend, there was good money to be made. It didn't appeal though we did need cash. We promised to think about it, let her know when we would join the other part-timers who travelled down the country most weekends, selling lines to supplement incomes or college grants.

"What's this fella's name again?" I was trying to keep up with Maeve as she strode up Rathmines Road, blue poncho flapping.

"Jeff, and I'm not asking him about the drugs – you can do that yourself."

Swallowing down the tightness in my throat, I felt the weight of the tape recorder against my thigh, standing behind her as she rang his bell.

"Maeve, how are you? Hi."

"This is Cathy, we were passing so we thought we'd call."

"Come in, it's so nice to see you," he seemed genuinely glad.

As we stepped inside a tall blonde woman, mid-thirties, stood smiling, waiting to be introduced.

"This is my girlfriend Sally, Sally meet Maeve and Cathy."

We struggled to look delighted, sitting down as requested, poised on the edge of the sofa, dismayed.

The kitchenette was part of the living room where Jeff stood putting on the kettle, offering tea. We accepted gratefully, eating his biscuits, conversation becoming laboured, pins and needles jabbing, on high alert, Maeve's eyes urging me to fulfil my mission.

The clock was ticking between silences, Sally's smile frozen, Jeff puzzled, looking from me to Maeve.

"We better be going then," I heard my voice, rising to go, Maeve behind me, disappointment, relief.

"Right, see ya Jeff, bye Sally, see ya again," Maeve tried to sound normal.

"What the hell was that all about? Why didn't you ask him?" her anger dissipating, seeing tears in my eyes.

"I just couldn't do it Maeve. I had to get out of there."

"Aye, I wasn't expecting a girlfriend."

"Me either, what now?" depression setting in.

Walking slowly, back on to Rathmines Road, reluctant to return to South Circular Maeve suddenly brightened.

"Do you know what we'll do?"

"What?" hope reappearing.

"We'll go up to John Kelly's flat; he'll do the interview for ya."

Originally from our parish, John had lived in Dublin for years, a national school teacher; his real passion was drama, starring in amateur plays all over the city.

"He'll be your ex drug addict, no better man."

She was right, he loved the idea, rehearsing his answers while he fed us with slabs of red cheddar on thick slices of homemade brown bread, laughing, getting into character, perfecting his middle-class Dublin accent. The cream cooker looking dangerously like ours, puffed and pettered as he lit the gas, setting three glasses on the table, beside the sugar, cloves, Johnny Walker red.

"We need to loosen up a wee bit girls before the performance."

Maeve, assigned to hot whiskeys, cigarette in mouth, waited for the kettle to boil; I pressed record, the interview began.

"Hello… Rod, I would like to know how you got into taking drugs." Maeve at the stove, stifling a giggle.

"Oh I was a crazy kid, you know, college was full of drugs so they seemed like a good idea at the time" his accent was awful, a cross between inner-city and the Bronx.

"What drugs were you addicted to?"

"Hell I was shootin' up all kinds o' stuff, snortin' too."

"Right. And what effect had the drugs on you?" the kettle began to whistle, Maeve still smirking, filling the glasses, stirring in sugar, placing steaming toddys on the armrests of our chairs.

"Well I would be on the bus in town and it would go round a corner and I would be wooo and wooo, wouldn't know where I was man."

"Right. That sounds awful," pressing the pause button, slurping our punch.

The taped discussion lasted two more hot whiskeys; all of us mildly inebriated by the time I said "Thank you so much Rod for telling me your story," pressing the stop button.

Replay, back to the beginning, we listened, drinking one more celebratory toddy, congratulating each other on a slick piece of work; Maeve and I waddled home, self-satisfied smiles, knowing this project would be top of the class.

Ethna was already home, three A4 pages of scrawled questions and answers on the table, she would write it up neatly later on. The alcohol had dulled my nasty symptoms, I went to bed confident of an easeful sleep, knowing there was a price to pay in the morning.

Undeterred by a magnified heartbeat, tightening throat, I sat in McGee's class the following Wednesday, introducing my project, pressing the play button. Fifty-two sets of ears listened, deadly silence, Rod's accent improbable, my pronunciation deteriorating, the whistle of a kettle, clink of glasses in the background, Rod now warbling, slurred thank you, a click, silence. Fr. McGee interrogated,seemingly convinced and I rallied, answering his probing questions surely, bravely and with conviction 'til he at last he relented, congratulating me on an insightful piece of work.

Afterwards, in the corridor, Joey was indignant, shouting loudly for all to hear, McGee somewhere in the crowd.

"Logue, you're a bleedin' chancer, he was no drug addict, I could hear a Donegal accent, that was some bloke you know."

Bile rose within me, fighting to sound nonchalant, I retorted "Now, now, Joey, jealousy'll get you nowhere."

"Yeah well you might have fooled Fr. McGee but you don't fool me."

The crowd had evaporated; I turned to face him, walking back quietly 'til our noses almost touched.

"Keep your fucking mouth shut you stupid wanker ya or I'll break your fucking face" hissing through clenched teeth.

He stood aghast, mouth open, unable to reply, shaking his head in disgust, he walked away; Ethna watched me, blinking off any hint of judgement as we joined the queue for lunch; I was starving.

January '79 ended on a high note; the Order of St. John of God were celebrating their centenary in March, our college along with the Clonliffe and All Hallows seminary was chosen to assemble the choir for the occasion. Sr. Bríd's voice quivered with excitement in the music hall Friday morning, impressing upon us what an honour it was that Seóirse Bodley had written the beautiful Mass of Joy especially for the commemoration; auditions would begin on Monday afternoon, only those with strong singing voices were invited to try their luck.

The geeks jumped up and down, spectacles steaming gleefully, convincing me to give it a miss until further details emerged in the foyer, pricking my antenna, giving me focus.

"It's on 8th March in St. Lawrence's Church, Kilmacud" Willie's teeth flashed, he always knew the minutiae.

"An awful lot of big names from the world of entertainment are attending, I heard daddy saying," posh Elaine from Dalkey.

"That's right," Willie's teeth again, "and there's a gala dinner in the Burlington afterwards with the Taoiseach, Garda Band, the lot."

The nasty symptoms were joined by a determined buzzing in my head, butterflies flapped in my tummy; I listened to them dogged, resolute, by God I would be in that bloody choir.

"Cathy, I haven't a note in my head." Ethna was refusing to join the auditionees lined up outside the music hall, Monday afternoon.

"Don't be silly, come on, you'll get through no bother, she'll make you sing do, re, mi, you'll be fine."

"Do you think?" she was relenting.

"Course, look if dopey drawers can do it so can you," we smiled sweetly at Willie, ahead of us in the line with the Clonliffe lads. I hoped the good looking, tall fella from Wales had an excellent set of pipes, indeed there was quite a smattering of handsome faces among those seminarians spurring my resolve, though I mourned their loss to the priesthood. We were brought in, in groups of ten the numbers were so large, Ethna mimed, I compensated, Bríd smiled, we were through.

Rehearsals began the following day, there wouldn't be a spare moment in February, voices soared, reverberating around the church of Clonliffe, the introductory hymn, the

Gloria,Hallelujah,Responsorial Psalm, the entire mass had to be learned, note perfect. We rose to the challenge, aware of its worth, the image of a gala dinner foremost in our minds, mixing with famous people, who knew what could happen?

Weekends were precious, giving us time to relax, catch up with Maeve, busy in college too, swotting for her degree. Rosie still managed to coax us into Garvey's occasionally, sparing me the humiliation of the talent contest, that fun had worn thin. I drank coca-cola most of the time, my appetite had increased since I stopped smoking; compensating with fish 'n' chips, Double Decker bars, Wagon Wheels, Chipsticks, bags of Golden Wonder, the weight piled on, my clothes felt uncomfortable. The weird feelings persisted, I battled silently, relatively secure in Maeve or Ethna's company though life had lost lustre, joy. Taking the bus across town became a constant trial, a flight or fight situation over which I was sometimes victorious, sometimes defeated. Ethna would patiently vacate the bus with me, never cross, a constant strong presence by my side that I leaned heavily on.

By the end of February the Seóirse Bodley Mass was coming nicely into shape. The mass of Joy was beautiful, uplifting. Standing in rehearsals I was free of the spiteful symptoms, released from their burden, my voice rang out strong, melodic, powerful. The notes of the hymn to St. John of God began, we responded. "The winter stones were sharp and clear…' Our enunciation crisp, concise, never taking our eyes off Sr. Bríd, her smile reassuring, giving confidence.

At least a dozen students from the class of '78 had made it into the choir, among them Joey and Willie. Joey had been giving me a wide berth, avoiding company where I was included, isolating himself more than me. A week before D-day Sr. Bríd instructed on dress etiquette, the ladies would wear white blouses, long black skirts, the men, white shirts, black trousers. The white blouse wasn't a problem, having received one in a parcel from my Aunt Mary in England, a high-necked lace Victorian replica that had been waiting for the right occasion. The black skirt was going to be difficult to source, perhaps the second hand stalls in the dandelion Market would come to my rescue. Ethna's cousin in Blackrock was lending her the blouse and skirt, being a bank manager's wife these garments were part of her staple wardrobe. With time running out I began to ask around, in the foyer and the canteen, hoping someone would come up trumps. Word of my predicament must have reached Joey's ears, giving him an opportunity for reconciliation, redemption.

"I hear you're looking for a black skirt for the choir," he stood beside me in the foyer, nervous, awkward, his body turned sideways.

"Yeah, so what?" I was prepared for some wisecrack.

"Me ma has one, I'll ask her for a lend if ya like."

"God that would be great, will it fit me?" suddenly I loved him.

"She's about your size, I'll bring it in tomorrow," he lolloped off down the corridor and I knew he was smiling.

The black velvet skirt fitted perfectly, flattering my expanding figure, complimenting the blouse beautifully. I admired myself in the mirror Monday evening, asking Maeve what she thought, delighted when she said I looked like Mia Farrow from The Great Gatsby.

Thursday March 8th had arrived, we took the bus across town early that morning, carrying our outfits with us, changing in college, applying makeup in the downstairs toilet. All staff who drove were offering lifts to Kilmacud; Ethna and I, along with two geeks piled into Fr. Weller's car, chatting politely, nipping Ethna in the back seat when geek number one announced she had joined the Legion of Mary.

We arrived an hour early, leaving time to get our bearings, have a final rehearsal, Sr. Bríd arranging us in order of height, ensuring my place in the front row, near the altar where my eagle eye could observe the burgeoning congregation. The top pews on either side of the main aisle were reserved for dignitaries and celebrities, although I didn't recognise most of them there were elbow jabs and whispers, when Dickie Rock arrived followed by Twink, I thought I saw Phil Coulter's handsome face though his name never surfaced in the post-event analyses. The altar swelled with hierarchy in crimson, purple, gold, black and white. Jack Lynch arrived taking his place in the front pew, a signal to begin, a hushed silence fell.

We stood as Archbiship Dermot Ryan led the procession, the organ notes rising strong and rounded, Sr. Bríd poised, ready to conduct. Our voices climbed, carrying the ceremony, moving through the Gloria, the Holy, Holy, raising the roof with the Great Amen, 'til we stood finally to sing the beautiful specially commissioned, recessional hymn, triumphant last line echoing, "but love will last eternally."

Victorious we stood, the entire congregation applauding loudly; turning to each other rejoicing, even Willie looked good, the geeks looked bearable.

Fr. Weller was on a high driving to the Burlington, stammering out his congratulations, smiling his excitement, me in the front beside him, smiling back anticipating the comfort of plush surroundings, sumptuous food, wine, warmth and fun. Miles of swirly carpet greeted us, tripping through revolving doors in our black and white, a sea of young penguins drawn to tables laden with hundreds of elegant little sherry glasses filled to the brim. The Clonliffe boys were already there with Joey and Willie drinking happily, laughing, posturing, watching those who passed by going directly into the function room, among them the Archbishop and the Taoiseach. Ethna and I took our places at the trough, knocking back the sweet liquid, feeling it coursing through our veins, gladdening our hearts, clinking glasses, giggling.

"Cheers big ears," winking at Ethna.

"Cheers queers and engineers," her favourite retort.

Joey and Willie sidled up followed by some of the handsome seminarians inviting us to sit with them for the meal, an honour we were delighted to bestow, following behind them, two full sherry glasses in each hand. Already giddy, we stood as the Papal Nuncio said grace, across the table from one another, pulling faces, squinting, trying to make Willie laugh so we could see his teeth. The waiting staff hovered, the Garda Band struck up a tune and the meal began. The sherries were dispatched quickly as the wine waiter made his way up the table repeating the most seductive question ever asked "red or white?" Glasses were replenished frequently, we elegantly disguised our greedy hunger among young men who took such bounteous food for granted in the seminary, where prawn cocktails, vegetable soup and roast beef, were served up on a regular basis. Baked Alaska scoffed I sang along with the music "these are a few of my favourite things" pointing at my wine glass, more clinking, talking loudly, jack Lynch speaking somewhere in the background.

Fr. Weller gestured to us, putting his index finger to his lips. Finally someone recited grace after meals bringing the evening to a close. Having left our belongings in the college that morning most of the choir had to trek across town, back to Drumcondra.

Loud and garrulous, we braved biting March winds, buttoning our coats to the chin. Darkness was falling on Leeson Street; we followed Pied Piper Willie, the sober one leading his merry troupe of classmates and seminarians, staggering along towards George's Street where the 16 bus ran. College was hosting an evening reception to honour our hard work, our dedication and we needed to retrieve our belongings, change out of our monochrome costumes. We invaded the bus, sitting upstairs, smoking, falling out of seats as we rounded corners. Ethna and I up front pretending to drive, all shouting 'wooo' 'yeeee' at every bend. Handbags fell to the floor, scattering lipsticks, purses, keys, triggering chivalry as giddy student priests went foraging, picking up contents, showing outstanding patience to plastered girls who shrieked each time, surprised that calamity had visited them.

Spirits still high, we charged the toilets, stuffing our white blouses and black skirts into plastic bags, eager to join the boys in the foyer, not wanting to lose momentum or the fun to end.

Vol-au-vents, sausage rolls in the canteen didn't entice, nor did glasses filled with orange juice or raspberry cordial. The handsome seminaries vanished along with Joey and most of our class, leaving Willie, still smiling, gnashers gleaming, nodding in our direction while he chatted sensibly to Sr. Marie Clare, a fellow classmate.

Sobriety was breaking through, dragging fatigue with it, fluttering fingers pressed around my throat. It was time to go home.

The bus pulled in at our stop, we dragged ourselves up the steps to 91, exhausted, empty, grieving that the day was now behind us. In unison we tried to relive the pomp, the grandeur of the event for Maeve in her pyjamas ready for bed. Hindered by the disinterest in her brown eyes we succumbed to fatigue, climbing into bed, the Garda Band still playing... "I simply remember my favourite things and then I don't feel so bad."

The following day was Friday, Ethna and I skipped college, hogging the beds 'til lunchtime. Maeve went home for the weekend, her mum would wash her dirty laundry, send her back Sunday evening sweet and pristine. Lack of money drove us out to Blackrock on Saturday, lured to lunch by Ethna's well-heeled cousin, we gorged on roast lamb, jelly and ice-cream, grateful when she asked us to stay the night, cosy in front of a coal fire watching Gay Byrne on the Late Late Show.

The flat felt colder, drearier on Sunday evening, sitting at the two-bar heater, putting on Rod, hoping he might cheer us up. "The Killing of Georgie" began, I had never really listened to the words before but I heard them now "Oh Georgie stay, don't go away..." tears ran down my cheeks, what a bloody gorgeous, sad song.

Maeve's key in the door shook away the dark feelings, delighted she had broken the spell I rose to put on the kettle, remembering we had homemade chocolate cake from Blackrock.

"How was your weekend? Any craic?" I handed her a mug of tea.

"It was quiet, I didn't really go out, bumped into Dan and Olly in the Sinn Féin shop," she took a quick look at Ethna.

"Oh yeah, how are they?" keeping my voice casual.

"Grand. They might be up again after Easter, another gig in The Meeting Place."

"Right," the casual sound was difficult to maintain.

"Oh listen, I want to give you a few of these" reaching into her rucksack Maeve produced what looked like a small bundle of rectangular fliers. She handed me one; staring out at me was the thin, bearded face of a young man sitting on a mattress, wrapped in a filthy looking blanket. The room was small, stark, with walls that appeared to have been daubed with an unknown substance. In black and white, a strangely compelling image with writing beneath the picture, explanatory bullet points.

"What is this?" a heavy feeling was making its way back.

"Read it," drama in Maeve's voice, "it explains what the men in the H-Blocks are going through," handing one to Ethna too.

We sat silently, reading about the dirty protest, the prisoners who wanted political status, the appalling injustices they endured, understanding then what the walls surrounding the bearded inmate were smeared with. Ativism summoned, rousing my rebel tendencies, I looked at Ethna hoping she felt it too, the same stab of anger, outrage.

"They're being treated like bloody animals," my voice shaking.

"How long will they keep this up?" Ethna was calm.

"Until the British Government reinstate political status and the privileges that go with it; they're prepared to go all the way with this."

"What do you mean, Maeve?" a shiver went through me.

"According to the boys in the Sinn Fein shop there's talk of hunger strikes, a lot of young men could die; we need to start putting pressure on our government to do something about this." She handed me another flier.

"Where do you want me to put these?" I knew Ethna wasn't moved by this cause, too dramatic for her as she handed the flier back to Maeve.

Ignoring Ethna's snub, she answered me in shades of Maud Gonne, urging me to action. "Put them up in college tomorrow on a notice board where they're obvious, you need to inform the students and staff about this, inform their minds, no more sitting on the fence."

Mind racing on the bus Monday morning, thinking about the young men in Long Kesh; Maeve's words playing over and over in my head. It was up to me to highlight the issue in college where no one seemed to know. It had never been raised during conversations in the foyer or the canteen, even rebel Betty seemed unaware of the situation. Preoccupied in Mr. Brennan's lecture, I missed his joke about Polonius' death behind the arras, whispering to Ethna as the class of '78 laughed.

"What did he say?"

"I said, Miss Logue, it was rather unnecessary of him to announce that he was slain!" peering over the rim of his black framed glasses. Now the centre of attention my face blazed, aware of sweaty palms, he held my gaze too long it seemed.

"Oh Miss Logue, Brennan has his eye on you," Joey's voice full of innuendo, heading for morning coffee after English.

"Shut up will ya," aware that some of the others were infected with his glee.

"Don't forget to give me back ma's skirt," we were queuing in the canteen.

"Yeah, it's in a bag downstairs, I'll give to to ya later."

The black and white flier impelled, I was wondering where to stick it. The canteen notice board caught my eye. Empty except for the coloured drawing pins, a prime location. I rooted in the bag, eager to achieve my mission. Ethna watched as I placed it, high up, sticking a pin in each corner.

"What do you think?" we were last in the queue now.

"Yeah, that looks fine," no real conviction in her voice.

Sitting where I could see the board, waiting for a crowd to gather, to hear shrieks of indignation, horror; nothing happened. The flier remained unread, the clock said it was time to go to Mc Gee's lecture, Sr. Marie Clare was presenting her project, Willie sprinted upstairs to room 2, eager to be of service to Miss 'goody two shoes.' Impressed by her offering Fr. McGee described it as beautifully sincere," a poignant interview with parents of a young boy with cerebral palsy,Phil Coulter's song "Scorn Not his Simplicity" woven cleverly thorough the dialogue adding credit, authenticity. Joey was staring at me, clapping loudly, I ignored him and clapped along with the others, raging I hadn't used Neil Young's "Needle and the Damage Done" as the backing track on my offering, Sr. Marie Clare did go up in my estimation.

Praise over, McGee released us to lunch, thankfully; permanently hungry now, my tummy rumbled, mouth watering at the thought of Betty heaping the plate with fish cakes and chips, hoping apple crumble and custard was on for dessert. The queue moved steadily along, the notice board came into view. It was empty.

"Jesus Ethna, where's the poster gone?" instant outrage.

Impatient, not waiting for her answer, my voice raised dangerously "Did anyone see the flier that was on the notice board here?" eyes darting around the canteen. Heads shook, some continued talking and laughing, shower of fuckers.

Heart pounding, jumping the queue, I confronted Betty.

"Betty, did you see the poster that was on the notice board after coffee this morning?"

"What poster?"

Ethna shouted, "Cathy it's here, look."

Reaching into the metal bin on the floor beneath the notice board she retrieved the discarded flier, still intact, fixing it to the original spot.

"Who the fuck did that I wonder?" hammering in my brain, paranoia jabbing.

"Maybe it just fell off, I don't know," her voice trailed.

"Fell off, my arse, who the hell has the right to do that?"

Taking our trays and sitting down, there was some comfort in seeing students, lecturers noticing the flier now, some reading closely, pointing at the image, talking in hushed tones to one another; good, perhaps my outburst had been effective.

"Did you find it?" Betty piled on the chips.

"Someone put it in the bin, the fucking cheek of them," defiance in my voice.

"Well I hope you wouldn't think it was me, Cathy."

"Jesus no, Betty, but I'll find out, don't you worry."

There were three empty chairs at our table, inviting posh Elaine, snobby Aishling, chinless Emmet to join us; they had noticed the flier, I couldn't resist.

"That's an awful situation in Long Kesh, isn't it?" challenging stare in my eyes.

"Was it you that put that poster up?" Emmet seemed amused.

"It certainly was, have you a problem with that Emmet?"

"Actually, I have a tremendous problem with the whole affair," posh Elaine, calm, confident.

"How do you mean?" my anger growing.

"I mean these guys are just murderers, guilty of killing hundreds of innocent people."

"That's right, common criminals," snobby Aishling chimed in, "political status indeed, hanging is too good for them."

Ethna squirmed nervously in her chair, sensing my exasperation, blinking rapidly, her eyes darting from face to face.

"But these young men are being treated like dogs, they're thinking of going on hunger strike, surely you don't agree with the British Government, Elaine" my voice incredulous.

"If they want to kill themselves that's their own business," she stirred her coffee, long elegant fingers beautifully manicured.

The down on Emmet's upper lip was visible in the sunlight, he grinned, enjoying the argument.

"I fucking can't believe you said that," control slipping away on me.

"Ah now lads, take it easy," Ethna's face flushed.

Insulted they rose to go, lifting their trays, snobby Aishling had the last word "I'm telling you Cathy, if Margaret Thatcher is elected Prime Minister in the upcoming general election in Britain she'll take no nonsense from those I.R.A. brutes, mark my words."

Ambushed, I ate my apple crumble aggressively, seething at Ethna's lack of passion or conviction, her failure to back me up and take my side.

"They're a shower of bitches, that Emmet's a wee prick."

"Pay no attention to them," she sounded tired, "come on, we better go up to philosophy."

Fr. Carmen purred, introducing us to Sartre's 'Existentialism of Humanism' walking around the room, his tone soothed; "man is nothing else but that which he makes of himself. That is the first principle…"

Fascinated I listened, released temporarily from angst, captured by his beautiful voice, all thought of hunger strikes banished until the wall clock said 4.30pm announcing afternoon tea. Fifty-two chairs scraped the floor, pushed back from desks in Room 3, most returning to the canteen before tutorials, hungry for coffee and biscuits.

Ahead in the queue Elaine was holding court, Aishling's head nodding while Emmet stole glances in my direction, displaying a wariness often reserved for the dangerously insane.

The notice board loomed; it was blank. The smirk on Emmet's face stung, bile rose again, swallowing hard, aware of the band tightening around my skull, I struggled to keep composure.

"It's not in the bin" Ethna's eyes anxious, handing me a tray.

"I'll ask Betty if she knows anything," tremble in my voice.

"It's not gone again is it?" she seemed genuinely puzzled.

"Are you sure you didn't see anyone taking it Betty?" tears in my eyes now.

"No, Jesus, sure I would have stopped them. I've been in the kitchen all afternoon so I wouldn't have noticed."

We sat, aware of Elaine at the next table surrounded now by a coterie of geeks, all nodding, all looking rapidly under their eyes in my direction, purposely loud voices:

"Common criminals…"

"Murderers…"

"Who cares…?"

"Here Logue, we'll go down to the foyer for a while" Ethna stacked our trays, rising, ignoring the clique forming, Betty's eyes following as we exited the canteen.

Oisín from fourth year was playing the guitar, we sat near him, listening to his voice, tremulous, a John Denver song, "It's cold here in the city, it often feels that way…."

Ethna lit up, inhaling deeply.

"Give me one of those," my resistance gone.

"Are you sure?" her eyes uncertain.

"Aye, I need one badly, it'll cure me or kill me," I tried to sound detached.

The chorus soared, "I'm sorry for the way things are in China…." sitting back enjoying the nicotine rush I'd been denying myself for weeks.

Gradually the foyer filled, students from all years, mostly smokers, listening to the music, quiet, convivial. Someone asked for another song as Oisín lit up himself. He handed the guitar to his classmate, Angie. More upbeat, she began "Rocky Raccoon, checked into his room, only to find Gideon's bible…" We sang along, "Duh, de du, du du, duh, de du, du…" spirits beginning to revive.

Quarter to six we rose to go as Fr. Weller descended the stairs, walking towards me, little smile, dancing eyes; feeling his customary squeeze of the elbow, his voice low.

"Would you come up to my office Cathy, if you're not in a hurry."

"Surely Father," looking at Ethna sitting down again, I followed him up the stairs, intrigued, nervous.

"Sit down, sit down, I won't keep you long" still smiling.

The room was warm and cosy, sitting in the black leather chair wondering what I'd done wrong.

"I believe you were upset today, Cathy, someone removed a poster you put up in the canteen?" concern in his voice.

"That's right, Father," deeply wounded now.

"Something to do with the men in Long Kesh, is that right?"

"I was just trying to highlight the terrible situation those prisoners are in, Father, no one seems to care or want to know."

"It's tragic, Cathy, tragic, very upsetting indeed, I agree with you," his smile replaced now by a mouth carved with sadness.

Sensitised, incredulous, I stared, silent.

"We feel so helpless on this side of the border, don't we Cathy, it's difficult to know what we can do; have you any ideas?"

Feeling placated and condoned, I was inspired, delicious revenge beckoning.

"Could we offer our class mass tomorrow morning for the men father, pray that a solution will be found to prevent them going on hunger strike, sure at least we can pray for them." Was there a halo over my head?

"That's a beautiful idea, Cathy, well done, we'll do that, you can pick the readings."

I rose to leave, feeling the gentle squeeze of the elbow, his voice saying "good girl."

Bounding down the stairs, signalling Ethna to follow, bursting with elation, I waited 'til we were on the Drumcondra Road to blab the exciting development.

"You won't believe this Ethna" she caught my eye encouraging me as we walked quickly to the bus stop.

"We're offering up the mass tomorrow morning for the men on the dirty protest, Fr. Weller's all for it" my voice pleading for reciprocation.

"Fair play to you Logue," she shared my delight, "you're going to make your point in style."

"Will you go in early with me tomorrow, I have to pick an O.T and N.T. reading and the gospel, imagine?"

"Course I will, here's the bus."

The evenings were stretching out, still light when we reached 91 South Circular. Rosie stood in the open doorway saying goodbye to a tall middle-aged man with glasses, buttoning his overcoat, walking briskly down the driveway. She waited in the hallway, Ethna slamming the front door behind us.

"Well girleens, what's the craic?"

She wanted to come in for a while and I was dying to hear her take on the Long Kesh situation.

"Fancy a cup of tea?" I knew she wanted one. Waddling in, limpedy-limp to her favourite chair; was it possible her arse was still expanding?

Maeve shouted to us from the kitchen, the kettle whistling in the background.

"Howyas, beans on toast anyone?"

"Hi Maeve," Ethna was kicking off her boots; "just three cups of tea would be lovely."

"Oh, howya Rosie," Maeve's head appeared, "three cups of tea coming up."

The crumpled ten pack of Gold Bond appeared then disappeared as Ethna proffered her pack of twenty Carrols; we lit up, relaxing, silent for a moment.

"There was some drama with that flier today, Maeve" intrigue in my voice, Rosie's eyes widening.

"Oh, do tell," Maeve calm, finishing her beans.

Ethna nodded in agreement, finishing off the odd word for me while I dramatised the events of the missing flier, the horrible attitude of Posh Elaine and Co., Fr. Weller's support and mass the next morning.

"Well good for you Logue, you highlighted the issue and you can do no more than that," Maeve, measured as usual.

"God I can't wait to see those wee bitches' faces tomorrow, it'll be some craic when they hear what the mass if for," there was still anger in my voice.

Rosie's eyes were dancing with devilment, "Do you know what you should do, Cathy, get up and give the sermon yourself, tell them posh fuckers that you have a flatmate in the I.R.A. and if they don't watch themselves she'll blow the shite outta the whole lot of them."

"And then I'll get Betty to sing James Connolly as the recessional hymn wearing a tricolour around her head."

Rosie's belly was jumping again, Ethna smiled weakly while I felt brief euphoric relief in hysterical laughter, tears on my cheeks.

"Now, now," Maeve cautioned, "don't get yourself too annoyed, you can't change how some people think. Just be dignified tomorrow and leave it at that."

Rosie changed the subject.

"Did ye give any more thought to coming out with us to make a few bob on the lines? What about this Saturday, we're heading down the country."

Suddenly we remembered that we were all heading home for the weekend.

"Not this Saturday, Rosie," Maeve, sensible, "it's Paddy's weekend. What about next Saturday, the 24th, would that suit?" She looked at all of us.

"I'll talk to John, the boss, I'd say that'll be fine, will ye all come out?"

"I'm asked to my cousin's in Blackrock that weekend" an urgency in Ethna's voice.

"We'll definitely go, won't we Logue?" Maeve nodded at me. I concurred.

We switched off the two-bar heater, as Rosie lifted her bottom out of the pink armchair, winking at me as she opened the door "Good luck tomorrow," red polo-neck, black skirt, bare legs moving slowly up the stairs, hovel door shut.

The bedroom felt cold as we pulled nighties over our heads; I needed the loo.

"Jesus I hate having to use this smelly hole" tying the belt of my dressing gown tight.

"Here, don't forget this," Ethna handed me the toilet roll, stolen from college earlier.

Finishing quickly in the cesspit I switched off the bedroom light, the girls already dozing.

"Ethna?" keeping my voice low, soft.

"Hym."

"We'll get up a bit earlier in the morning; we need time to pick the readings."

"I've my clock set for seven," that was final.

I fell asleep, the words of James Connolly going round and round in my head.

The college library was already warm and cosy at eight o'clock; Ethna sitting opposite me, ransacking the

Old Testament, me hunting through Matthew's gospel, a particular passage in mind, where the hell was it?

Found it, Matthew 7:1-5, Fr. Weller would be reading this, he was no fool. I was sure he'd get the point.

"Any luck there Mullins?"

"I don't know what I'm looking for."

"Something about war or the law, enemies, anything that will stick it to these smug goody goodies, bloody well think they're so perfect" my voice impatient.

"I'll try the New Testament so," she sounded purposeful, "you look in the Old Testament, you'll have better luck than me."

At 9 o'clock we glimpsed Fr. Weller making his way towards us, smiling, head bobbing, we smiled back, assured and ready.

"Cathy, Ethna, good morning, readings chosen?"

"Yes Father" I talked, Ethna nodded. "This is your gospel reading" handing him the Bible, "I'll read the Old Testament passage from Psalm 71 and Ethna is reading from Roman Chapter 7.

"Wonderful girls, wonderful," quick squeeze of my elbow, "see you in the chapel."

By 9.25am the class of '78 had gathered in their usual cliques, filling the small church, sitting in their usual places except for Ethna and I who sat at the front where Wilie and Sr. Marie Clare usually perched. Downgraded two rows behind us looking mildly disgruntled, Willie blinked hard, licking his teeth in time with the blinking.

Bonyarse Emer from Carlow with the fake plummy accent was handing out hymn sheets, thinking she had a great voice, sing fuck all as far as I was concerned.

Joey was helping Emmett prepare the altar, lighting candles, smoothing cloths, setting bread and wine on a little side table; look at them, they wouldn't know a joint if it jumped up and bit them on the arse. Geeks abounded, taking up the front, the middle, oddballs, rebels and misfits near the back, there because the geeks felt entitled to be up the front, Pharisees.Fr. Weller was well aware of the pecking order. The entrance hymn began, "Now thank we all our God..." we stood, bonyarse screeching somewhere, Fr. Weller kissing the altar, white alb moving to the lectern, he spoke.

"Morning, welcome everyone..." my heart pounding violently, "we are offering our mass this morning for the men in Long Kesh prison, our brothers in Christ who find themselves in pain and suffering. We ask God in his wisdom to come to their aid, helping all involved to bring about a just resolution to this tragic situation, let us pray..."

Heads bowed, I stood tall, shoulders back, head hoisted by an invisible magnet above. I remembered Maeve's words, resisting the urge to look behind defiantly, hearing Ethna's breathing deep and warm beside me.

"Now we'll have our first reading," the call to arms.

I stepped onto the altar opening the Bible where the page was marked. "A reading from Psalm 71." Band tightening round my head, hands wet dampening the delicate pages, Jesus let me do this right, come on Logue.

"Deliver me, O my God out of the hands of the wicked...speak against me and those who lie in wait for my life counsel together... O my God, make haste to help me," Stressing certain words, accent heavily northern. Well done Logue, sit down now; Ethna rising as I sat, pins and needles surging, focus on Ethna now, her voice very southern, what odds, she sounds confident, calm, good on you Mullins.

"A reading from the Letter of St. Paul to the Romans… "therefore my brethren, you have become dead to the law through the body of Christ… we have been delivered from the law… not in the oldness of the letter. This is the word of the Lord."

"Thanks be to God."

Stoic, standing beside me again, I whispered quickly, "Brilliant."

"The gospel according to Matthew" we made the sign of the cross, foreheads, lips and chests.

"Judge not, that you be not judged, for with that judgement you judge, you will be judged… and why do you look at the speck in your brother's eye but do not consider the plank in your own eye?...." Will I look over at them now to see their faces, better not, Fr. Weller's eyes were on me, had to keep my halo in place.

"This is the gospel of the Lord."

"Praise to you Lord Jesus Christ," was I shouting?

His homily, based on the readings, unwittingly fed my intentions, Shakespearian in theme, he reminded us that not all laws are just, there is a higher power we must sometimes follow; there was a difference between killing for a cause and dying for a cause; he mentioned martyrs, cited Ghandi, Martin Luther King, asking us finally to pray for a speedy resolution, no more lives should be lost.

We stood for the recessional hymn "Today is the day that the Lord has made let us rejoice and be glad."

Bonyarse still screeching in the background.

Ethna seemed excited "Ah Cathy, that was fantastic…"

"Shou! Don't give them the satisfaction, come on up to the altar and thank Fr. Weller, quick."

"Well I hope it does some good, Cathy," holding my hand in his, eyes twinkling, rabbiting on, Ethna nodding, smiling back, class of '78 filing out, chastened, stung.

The smell of coffee beckoned, for once I wasn't starving; we joined the end of the queue behind Joey and Emmet who seemed inordinately friendly, respectful even. Ethna and I withholding subtly, they weren't going to bask too easily in our new found validation.

The Southside snootys were already seated, posh Elaine holding court, eyes downcast, frowning, snobby Aishling looking like a fish out of water, mouth opening and closing but no sound. Looking up they caught my eye, the taste of sweet revenge filled my mouth, sliding down my throat like nectar unimpeded by tightening bands or choking sensations. I pursed my lips, gazing at them with patronising eyes, smiling, a parody of scrumptious charming delight, beaming, my head moving from right to left like a cute little old lady. Flummoxed, they reached for their coffees; Betty came into view giving me the thumbs up for a job well done, and I realised in that instant she had informed Fr. Weller about the missing flier orchestrating my triumph.

"Coffee Ms. Logue?" all business.

"Yes please Betty and a slice of your best apple pie."

"Would you like that heated me dear?"

"No Betty, I think today it's best served cold."

She laughed, handing me a generous slice.

Aware of many eyes on us, I followed Ethna to the last two vacant chairs, sitting with Willie and Sr. Marie Clare, who seemed delighted with our company, Willie's teeth flashing in deference, Marie Clare complimenting our readings, appropriate and insightful she thought.

We floated along in a haze of glory, reluctant to leave college at 4 o'clock, lectures over 'til Monday, bags needed packing though, we donned coats and headed to the bus stop.

I better start buying cigarettes I thought, Ethna handing me a Carroll, the conductor making his way down the aisle clanking out tickets, recognition in his eyes.

"We'll pay the full fare," giving Ethna the knowing look.

"Yes ladies, where are we off to, South Circular by any chance?"

"Sure we might as well, I believe it's lovely up there," I handed him the 22p, correct fare, laughing, watching Ethna doing the same. Failing to ignite humour, he handed us the tickets sour, silent.

Looking through grimy windows, blowing out inhaled smoke slowly, luxuriously the bus turned onto South Great George's Street, an elegant older woman hurried towards Dunnes Stores wearing a black velvet skirt, the breath caught in my throat.

"Oh fuck, Jesus, I'm in trouble."

"Is it happening again? Will we get off?" Ethna's green eyes piercing.

"No, no, I'm not having a panic attack; I forgot to give Joey back his mother's skirt."

"That was ages ago, he'll have forgotten all about it by now," she looked relieved.

"Oh he'll not forget, he'll hound me wait 'til ya see."

"Where is it anyway?"

"It was in a plastic bag, I threw it under one of the chairs in the foyer."

"It'll be long gone by now, Logue," she sounded delighted.

The train to Cork pulled out of Heuston at 10 o'clock the following morning, Ethna on it, Norma picking her up as usual. Maeve and I headed to Bus Aras, no hitching this time, still recovering from our lucky escape at Christmas, we'd wait 'til the days were long and bright before sticking out our thumbs again.

The dismal atmosphere at home prevailed. Mum's inquisition instant, the cheques I'd written since December had arrived in the post.

"What did you write this one for... You seem to be spending a lot on groceries... I thought you told me the new coat was only £4?" relentless. Malachy wouldn't be home, he was spending the weekend with a friend in Buncrana.

On Paddy's Day the chimney went on fire, I had to run and get Tony our neighbour, seeing as dad was on the piss, missing, not that he would have been any good even if he was there. Decent, reliable Tony came to the rescue armed with wet towels and a big board which he held in front of the fireplace to stop the burning soot falling on the carpet. Mum, pale and shaken begged me not to go out for the day; a car load was heading on a pub-crawl around Letterkenny, it would be great craic.

Hampered, I stayed with her, imagining the others laughing, chatting, drinking their way round the town, not missing me one little bit; always the outsider.

By 3 o'clock Sunday dad still hadn't returned, I was grateful when Maeve's mum beeped the horn at 4o'clock taking us to the bus station. Relieved to get away, not hearing his terrible anger, not seeing the sad, haunted look in mum's eyes.

"Well what kind of time did ye all have?" Rosie on her throne, us huddled around the heater, both bars glowing, Ethna, Maeve and herself watching, listening; me regailing them with the hilarity of our chimney on fire and dad away, pissed somewhere and me and mum standing shaking like two eejits waiting for the whole fucking house to go up. Rosie's belly jumping, snorting, Gold Bond in hand. Rod singing 'Keep me Hanging On' worn out with the fun of it all.

"You're a craic, Logue," Maeve unconvinced.

"How was your weekend, Rosie?" Ethna changing the subject.

"Quiet. Went to Garveys with Pat and Dominick Saturday evening for a few, twas jammed, couldn't get a seat, I wasn't fit to be standing all night with this gammy leg of mine.

"Were you born with that?" Ethna's matter of fact tone embarrassed Maeve. Rosie didn't seem to mind.

"No, I was in a serious car accident when I was 15, nearly died, touch and go, limping since."

"Jesus. God," we sounded suitably shocked.

"Sure I'd be lost without the taxis," she winked, breaking tension, we laughed again.

"So we're still all set for Saturday?" she raised her eyebrows.

"Oh yeah, sure are, except for Ethna," I answered, noticing a little smile curling at the corners of Ethna's mouth.

"Where down-the-country Rosie?" Maeve stubbed her butt in the dirty ashtray, a present from Garvey's.

"I haven't a bloody clue, the boss'll make all that clear when he picks us up Saturday morning; we'll be out on the road early, around 9." She exited, leaving behind an odour that wafted unkindly from the faded pink armchair.

"The skirt's not the only thing she doesn't change" I grimaced, spraying the offending seat generously with Charlie perfume. Maeve rubbed her hands gleefully, scrunching up her nose, Ethna looked disgusted.

We unpacked, putting clean towels, freshly laundered clothes back in our wardrobes, comforted at the sight of homemade bread, a cooked chicken, coming out of Ethna's rucksack; fair play to her aule doll.

Tucked into beds, drifting off to our private worlds I found it hard to sleep, listening to the traffic, anxiety symptoms ever present, surging at the memory of a misplaced skirt, dozing eventually, wishing the morning was days away.

By Friday my periphery vision was so heightened I could spot Joey coming at a hundred yards. Any hint of a blue jumper propelled me in the opposite direction, Ethna following me bemused; skulking behind pillars, under stairs, darting into the ladies, standing at the sinks till Ethna signalled the coast was clear.

"This will have to stop, Cathy," smoking with Oisín in the foyer, hoping he'd play something on the guitar.

"He'll go off the head, that was an expensive skirt," annoyed that I might have to replace it.

"Just tell him the truth," nudging me hard, the blue jumper stood above me, heart pumping, I was cornered.

"Logue," sounding sarcastic, "you never gave me back me ma's skirt."

"Sure I told ya where it was, remember?" standing now, Ethna watching the performance.

"What you said was you had it in a bag and you would give it to me later," shaking his head. "You lost it, didn't you? I bleedin' knew it," disgusted.

"I told ya to go down and get it in the foyer under the black chair" feigning exasperation. He turned, waving his hand in the air, head still shaking, walking away; he was through with me.

The 16A stuttered up Harrington Road in rush hour traffic, Ethna had been quiet since we left college, refusing cigarettes, saying she was smoked out. Seeming impatient to get away, she threw a few tings into her rucksack in the bedroom, speeding up when she heard raucous laughter in the hall, Rosie talking to Dominic on his way in from work, heading to his flat downstairs in the basement.

"Fancy some scrambled egg 'n' toast before ya go?"

"No, there'll be dinner for me in Blackrock, can't wait, she'll have a big fire on, the double bed made up."

"Ya lucky duck."

"I know. Right, I'm off, good luck tomorrow."

Maeve passed her in the hallway, delighted to see I was in, kettle on, heater on, meter knifed full, Rod's gravelly voice rising… 'You're in my heart, you're in my soul…" Around 8 o'clock the doorbell rang, Rosie, Dominic, Pat inviting us to Garvey's for a few drinks on Pat, there was music upstairs as usual Friday night.

Maeve in her knee-length polo neck looked doubtful, "I don't know, Rosie, we have to be up early, be in good form tomorrow."

"One drink won't kill ye, come on, we'll get young Logue up for a few songs" limpy limp to the front door in her black leather jacket before we could reply.

Six drinks later we were flying, organ grinder out of tune, some aule biddy singing The White Cliffs of Dover, Rosie saying it would be a blessing if God took her and threw her off the bloody cliffs. Vodka and cokes all round, doubles when the bell rang for last orders, the two lads staggering back to the table managing to keep most of the liquid in the glasses.

An atom of sense prevailed, refusing to go to the Garda Club, we waved the boys off, heading instead to the chipper for fish suppers, eating them at Rosie's kitchen table, immune temporarily to the foul aroma.

The phone woke us at 8 o'clock, hangovers ignited, instantly aware of throbbing heads, heavy stomachs; we dragged ourselves moaning out of bed, hearing Rosie's voice in the hall, rapping the door, and shouting.

"That was John, the boss, get outta the scratchers girleens, get your knickers on, he'll be here at 9."

We dressed clumsily, wrapped up against the presumed cold, repulsed by the thought of tea or toast, waiting like condemned prisoners, painfully regretting the night before.

John took his job seriously, standing inside the front door arming us with clipper boards, pink cards with Support Autistic Children printed in red at the top. We followed him down the path, Meave in her poncho and beret, me cocooned in Ethna's green duffel coat, shivering, orphans after Bill Sikes; Rosie with the bare legs, limpedy limp, him in his camel coat, mohair scarf, leather gloves. Probably in his early forties, tall, short brown hair, dark glasses, he seemed friendly enough, outlining our itinerary, holding open the back door of his big plush car. The front seat was already occupied by Vera, joining us on the expedition, experienced in the ranks, Rosie had met her before. Comforted by the warmth, the luxury, I tried to relax, enjoy the journey, driving out of the city, leaving built up areas behind, first time on the Naas Dual Carriageway. Maeve chose well to get in first I thought, leaving me in the middle, Rosie's bulk weighing heavily on my left side, a mixture of stenches rising periodically, drifting, lingering briefly, fading, followed quickly by reserves.

"Do you mind if I put down the window for a minute John?" her voice startled me. Jesus she can't even put up with the stink herself.

"No problem, actually I'll put off the heater for a while, it might be getting too warm in the back there girls."

"Could you pull in John, I'm going to be sick," her voice urgent and her hand already on the handle, up ahead a road sign said Kill. We swerved, stopping just in time, back door hanging open, retching sounds, Rosie leaning, near the petrol cap. No one else moved, staring ahead we listened, breaks between retching, moaning 'Oh God', 'fuck me', more spewing, a few 'ohs' in succession, then limpedy-limp, back in the car, door slammed tight.

"Sorry about that folks, the aule fish supper didn't sit right."

Vera handed back some tissues, she wiped her mouth, spreading out again, a new stench joining the reserves, Maeve pinched my thigh, I knew she was sniggering silently out the window.

Resuming our journey, John switched on the radio, 10 o'clock news, all bleak, depressing: PAYE demonstrations, a raft of I.R.A. bombings all over Northern Ireland. I rubbed my sweaty palms along the velvet upholstery wishing I could inhabit Maeve's body, even Vera's, shed this one of mine with pumping heart, dry mouth, tight throat, evil pins and needles threatening, pitiless bastards. A shower of rain stabbed at the windscreen, the sun was lost in the grey sky; Rosie's breath stale, rhythmic near me, Maeve studying the cards, determined to be the top seller, make lots of money.

The landscape was building up again, a road sign announced Portlaoise two miles, time to face the trenches, someone kill me now.

Off the Dublin Road into Main Street, John pulled over, the car still running, giving the final instructions. "Right Rosie, Cathy, this is where you get off. Rosie you stand here at the bottom of the street, Cathy you walk up, place yourself outside Penneys. Now look pleasant, engage the people, display your permits, talk about the prizes and sell as many lines as possible between now and six o'clock. It's a Saturday so it'll be busy, take a break around 2 o'clock and remember you get £10 for every card you sell. We'll go on to Roscrea, pick you up here at 6 o'clock on the dot. Good luck."

A spiteful wind bit, walking slowly, watching John's car moving into the distance, reneging feet moving one past the other.

"Will you walk up to Penneys with me, Rosie?"

"Go on outta that, sure you can see it from here. You'll be grand."

Cars parking, unparking, from the row along main street, a firing squad I stood facing with my clipper board, cards and biro, this day would last forever.

"Help support autistic children please" too quiet, no one was responding, I raised the volume considerably. "Autistic children, please help support autistic children, please!"

"How much are they pet?" an old dear in a shabby green coat with a brown fur collar.

"They're 50p a line". There were thirty lines on the card. She bought one, telling me her name, address, wondering what she would win as my trembling fingers scrawled her details on line No. 7.

"The draw takes place on May 26th; the winner gets a brand new Ford Escort."

By 12 o'clock only lines 1, 3 7 were sold, no one cared about autistic children, neither did I.

An old black bug of a car spluttered up the street, turning into a vacant space only feet away. Dung splattered wellington emerged followed by another, round squat body, mutton head in an ancient crombie held closed in the middle with cord. Shoulders hunched forward, approaching, shouting "What did you say them tickets is for?"

"They're for autistic children, 50p a line" pins and needles on high alert.

"And where would these handicapped childers be from?"

"Ahm... Dublin... and that..." wrong fucking answer.

"Is that right now, well we have ortistic childer down here too ya know" turning, snorting, heading back to the jalopy, opening the passenger door, helping her out. I watched in a fog, Lambeg drum beating in my head.

Oh no, oh Jesus no, will I run away up the fucking street. Pushing her gently along, exhibit one, four foot nothing, weighing in at fifteen stone, eyes bulging, wheezing in motion, tongue hanging loosely on lower lip.

Back on her perch Rosie reached for the half smoked Gold Bond, still lit in the ash tray, a prayer in my heart that consternation was over for the day.

Giving me a furtive sideways glance, exhaling, she spoke.

"I suppose you know what's wrong with me?"

Cymbals clashed again, staring, noticing the flecks of gold in her pupils, full lips moving slyly, almost smiling.

"Are you pregnant?" please say no.

"Eight months," announced with proud belligerence.

Palpations, invisible neck brace tightening.

"Will ya be able to stand for the rest of the day selling lines?" please say yes, go away, leave me alone.

"Oh Jesus," she was doubling over.

"My God, what's wrong Rosie, Oh my God!" bolt upright now my hand on her shoulder.

"I'm getting fierce pains and the wee fucker is kicking the shite outta me." Recovering slightly.

"Do ya think you're in labour?" cold sweat in my armpits.

"Feels like it alright, oh holy fuck," grabbing her large distended belly, how had I not noticed this, none of us had, we must be stupid.

"Come on, we'll have to find the hospital," helping her down off the stool, cutlery suspended again, conversations slowed, eyes staring as we threw some change on the counter, made our way to the door.

Outside in the unfriendly wind she grabbed me, "I'm not going to any bloody hospital, no way."

"What are we going to do then, what if the baby is coming?" panic in my voice, shivering to the roots of my hair.

"There's no way I'm going into a hospital, I know that much. Oh, oh, Jesus!"

Terror was taking hold, the sound of a siren in the distance gave a glimmer of hope, inspiring me.

"Right, I know what we'll do, we'll find the police station, ask the Guards for help."

She didn't protest. Grateful, I turned right, walking aimlessly, no one around to ask directions, Rosie limping beside me, pale, stalling.

We turned off Main Street, on a narrower road, eyes darting, searching for a building that looked like a Garda station, stopping at intervals, Rosie bending over, holding walls, gasping and cursing.

"Excuse me, could you tell me where the Garda station is please?" appealing to a middle-aged woman with a kind face.

"You're on the wrong street dear, this is Railway Street, you need to turn, head back towards Main Street, take a left and go onto Abbeyleix Road, the station is up there a bit," her eyes watching Rosie all the while.

We set off, wind easing, sun trying to make an appearance in the grey sky, a sense of purpose now.

"Come on Rosie, we know where we're going at last" I almost sounded joyful.

"I'm doing me best; oh Christ! Hold on, hold on" leaning on someone's window sill, heaving, muttering, "this fucker has me kicked senseless, I'm telling you you'll get some fucking kicking when you come out, just wait me boyo!"

The going was slow, laborious, constant stops while Rosie writhed, face contorted, muttering, cursing, threatening her unborn child with a selection of punishments upon its arrival. Me on high alert waiting for the promised land to appear in a blaze of glory. Snail-like, hindered, watching her hobbling behind me, noticing a pub on the opposite side of the road.

"Listen, why don't you wait there," nodding towards the bar, "rest yourself and I'll run on up and find the station."

The idea appealed to her so we crossed the wide thoroughfare a delivery lorry pulling away, Guinness written on the side. A row of silver barrels stood sentry, one with Rosie's name on it.

"I'll sit here and wait, I'm not going into a pub on me own."

OK, don't move from this spot" walking away quickly, almost running, where is this fucking station. Legs taking control, sprinting, head swivelling on 180° axis, it appeared, gargantuan and palatial. A heavenly choir sang, shafts of sunlight beamed stopping me in my tracks, I stared at deliverance before me. The arched entrance announced 'Garda Síochána', impressive white building, daunting, squad cars parked outside, heart thumping, moving under the arch, nearly there.

A young Garda emerged, dapper in full uniform, silver buttons flashing, purposeful, now's your chance Logue, go on, go on.

"Excuse me Guard, could you help me please?" his hand on the handle of the car door, in a rush. "You see my friend is down the road, she's in trouble, I think she's going to have a baby any minute and she doesn't want to go to hospital and…"

Brow furrowing, hand raised defensively, he interrupted.

"Hold on a minute now, I'm not the one you need to speak to. Come inside, I'll get the sergeant to deal with you."

Hot on his heels I followed, mixed emotions, was I being rescued, maybe I'd be held on some strange charge, in possession of a bare-legged, limping pregnant woman, smelly and unmarried.

"Take a seat there; I'll have a word with Sergeant Mahony."

I sat on a long wooden bench in reception, taking in my surroundings, pleasant, modern area, big windows, light, no female Guards, males only, walking around, all checking me out, staring, why are they looking at me like that?

Big round clock on the wall, ticking, 2.15pm, poor Rosie sitting on that cold barrel, heat seeping into my bones, feeling guilty, why was he taking so long?

I heard footsteps first, heavy, deliberate on the tiled floor, raising the volume of my heartbeat, he rounded, tall and bulky and pugnacious.

"Now young lady, what's this nonsense you were telling one of my men, something about a pregnant girl?" Bending towards me, his face shoved close displaying blue veins on a red bulbous nose, hands behind his back.

"That's right Sergeant, I'm along with this girl and I just found out she's pregnant, she's in labour and doesn't want to go to hospital, I really need help," voice starting to break, tears stinging.

"All right, all right," his tone softening, sitting beside me, a long hard-backed ledger in one hand, biro in the other.

"Now I'm going to have to ask you some questions and you're going to answer me honestly, we'll see then what we can do" this was going to take a while.

"But Sergeant, she's sitting outside a pub down the road there, she could have the baby any minute," tears flowing now, dam burst.

"Never mind that now for the time being," opening the statement book, writing in the date, day, time.

"Your full name please?"

"Cathy Logue," sobbing.

"Where are you from Cathy?" businesslike.

"County Donegal," slight sob.

"What are your parents' names?" concentrating on his writing.

"Jim and Gracie," vague bewilderment.

"Brothers or sisters?"

"One brother," this is stupid.

"His name?"

"Malachy," oh come on.

"Have you or any of your family ever been in trouble with the law?" eyes staring, mouth pursed, waiting for my reply.

"No!" exasperation building.

"Your friend's name is?" ignoring my agitation.

"Rosie Diver, she's not really my friend" opening a whole new can of worms.

"And where is she from?" no change in his expression.

"Limerick."

"How many in her family?"

"Eight, she has a sister living in Dublin," calming down now.

"What's her sister's name?"

"Grainne," and she's a dab hand at swapping price tags.

"Do you know her address?"

"I just know she lives in Clondalkin," for fuck's sake.

"What's your address in Dublin?"

"91 South Circular Road," it's a kip.

"Who's your landlord there?"

"Mr. Tommy Heenan, we don't see him much, I know nothing about him except he drives a cream Mercedes Benz" and he's a mean ole bollocks.

"Who else lives with you?"

"A girl from Cork called Ethna Mullins" lucky bitch "and a girl from home, Maeve McLaughlin, we went to boarding school together," please don't start asking me about that.

"And Rosie Diver lives in the house too?"

"Yeah, she's in the flat upstairs" a complete hovel.

The quiz continued, younger Guards still coming and going, watching me, a curiosity, heads peering round corners, disappearing, Sergeant Mahony writing furiously into his notebook, fat, hairy fingers, wide gold wedding band.

Rosie sold lines for a living, for autistic children, her boss was John, that's all I knew about her, wasn't telling him about creepy men passing through the hall at night or her trick with the taxis.

"Do you know if Rosie Diver has a criminal record?" the firing shot.

"I don't think so Sergeant, she never mentioned anything like that," never entered my mind.

"Right, that'll do for now, I'll round up a few of the lads so, we'll go down and meet Miss Rosie Diver," closing his notebook, leaving me sitting, waiting for a few more minutes. Drifting back to thoughts of Rosie on the cold beer barrel, he stood signalling to me. I rose, two young Guards walking quickly through the front doors, down the steps, getting into a squad car, both in the front, me in the back, Sergeant Mahony pushing in beside me closing the door.

My mind like a big freight train flying down the tracks, I'm in a squad car, safe, but ashamed, what if someone spots me, like all the people who saw me earlier selling lines on Main Street, they'll think I'm a criminal. What if Rosie's gone, why does yer man in the passenger seat keep looking around at me, the driver keeps peering in the rear-view mirror. Passing out under the grand arch back on Abbeyleix Road, Lambeg drum trying to make a comeback. Silence, driving along, the pub in the distance, visible, in focus, there she sat, a brooding hen, stumpy legs not touching the ground, unconcerned, not a care in the world.

"Is that her?" jutting his head between the two front seats.

"Yeh, that's her," she almost looked contented.

"Pull over lads. Now you stay here Miss Logue, let me talk to her first."

She watched his approach, sitting relaxed, standing over her Sergeant Mahony's right hand gesticulating, Rosie's head nodding, hint of a grin, quizzical expression on her face, more nodding as he moved closer to her, a silent movie without music, only the rapid throbbing of my heart. Enthralled, the three of us sat attentively, seeing her shifting her weight, dismounting laboriously, limpedy-limp after the sergeant as he held open the car door inviting her to join us in the back seat. Stout black brogues appeared followed by purple heat-patterned legs, dragging in the rest of her bulk, fat arse edging along into the middle, panting, and the sergeant in behind her slamming the door, giving directions at the same time.

"Grand lads, up to the hospital."

"How's it going boys?" Rosie's voice casual.

No reply from the front, driver's eyes in the rear-view mirror. Reaching into the pocket of her leather jacket she produced the crumpled ten pack of Gold Bond, "Any of you boys smoke?" Silence, Guard in the passenger seat turning to look at her, driver taking her in again in the rear view mirror.

"Jesus I'm outta matches, anyone have a light?" putting a cigarette in her mouth. No reply. From somewhere came a low giggle, getting louder, louder, then hysterical, uncontained chortling, chest heaving, volcanic, tears flowing down my cheeks, infecting the two young Guards who smirked stifling guffaws, Rosie's belly now jumping, delighted to be so amusing. Sergeant Mahony looking on mouth open, nonplussed. "Now when we get up here I'll go in and have a word with the matron" trying to restore sanity.

All nodding, delighted to comply, Rosie trying to communicate something out the corner of her mouth to the effect of "not going into fucking hospital" repeated over and over.

Pulling up at the main entrance Mahony alighted, walking swiftly inside, his door swinging open, cold air intruding, looking at Rosie's side face, noticing the yellow pallor of her skin.

"Excuse me boys, sorry about this," she jostled hoisting herself through the open door, outside, bending near the boot, loud retching sounds, unburdening herself amid gulps, gasps, curses, the two in the front sniggering at each other, sniggering at me.

Mahony back at the entrance, accompanied by a young nurse wielding a wheelchair, his big beefy hand gesturing to Rosie, a springing heifer, stubborn, standing her ground, the sergeant losing patience, big frustrated head on him striding towards us.

"Come on now like a good woman, we have a nice bed for you inside, you'll be well looked after."

He was going to need help convincing her. I got out, casual, stood beside her, offering a cigarette, lighting up, watching Mahony's backside, leaning in talking to his driver through the open window.

"He has another thought coming if he thinks I'm going into that place" determination in her voice. "Look at yer one with the wheelchair; I'll wrap it around her fucking head if she comes anywhere near me with it."

"Sure maybe it would be no harm to go in for a wee while Rosie, they'll just give you a check up, make sure everything's all right," using my gentle persuasive tone.

"I hate bloody doctors proddin' and pokin'," she made a distasteful face.

"How many checkups did ya have so far?"

"None."

"None?" incredulous, "ah Jesus Rosie, come on now, go in and let them take a wee look at you, for God's sake," desperation creeping in.

Throwing her cigarette to the ground, black brogue stamping it out, she looked unsure, glancing at Mahony, thinking, a cold wind blowing, the young nurse still rooted behind the wheelchair, shivering, patient.

"Sergeant Mahony, I think Rosie is ready to go in now," I took a chance.

"Good, good woman," relieved, waving the nurse over, Rose and I meeting her halfway.

Gratitude welled up inside me, helping her to sit, releasing the break, being wheeled backwards through automatic doors, a sudden change of mind gripped her as I stood smiling, waving.

"I don't want to go in, I'm not staying here, I'm not staying here!" fading as she moved down the corridor, blissfully ignoring her, I continued waving and smiling. She vanished round the corner; I turned towards the sliding doors.

Mahony beside me, complicit, the squad car still running, two anxious faces watching as we walked towards them, fearful that Rosie would emerge, bolting, steam rising, charging at them. My clipper board lay on the floor, causing a sinking sensation, tinging my joy, tugging at the rug of comfort beneath me. Eagle-eyed, the sergeant aware of the changing atmosphere came again to the rescue.

"You'll come back to the station with us, we all need a cup of strong tea after that, don't we boys?" winking at the young guns in the front, pushing in beside me, warm and comfortable, driving out the hospital gates.

"Stick on the radio there Colm 'til we get the 3 o'clock news," rubbing the heat back into his jumbo fingers, Mahony seemed jubilant.

Déjà vu driving down the Dublin Road, back up Main Street past Pennys, heart beginning to drum a little, catching sight of the black bug parked in a new spot further up the street: shoppers staring as we drove along.

The newsreaders voice distracting; the IRA were responsible for the assassination of the British Ambassador to Holland.

"Surprise, surprise," the driver's voice, low and sarcastic.

"They've had some week of it, twenty-four bombs in the North, they're destroying the place," shotgun Garda sounded pleased with himself.

"And no doubt we'll get more of them down here, looking for special conditions, drawin' Amnesty International on us," they were in full flight.

Sergeant Mahony remained silent, rubbing his hands again as we drove past Rosie's empty barrel, indicating, turning right under the arch, pulling up at the station door, what now I wondered.

"Come into the canteen, we'll get a nice cup a tae," his fingers on the door handle.

Reaching for the clipper board I followed him, the young guns close behind him, hunger rattling my stomach hankering for something sweet. We parted ways in the hall, only the sergeant and myself needing sustenance. The canteen was spacious and empty, Mahony all business directing me to sit, taking my order, arriving back with black tea for me, a milky looking affair for himself, throwing down a selection of bars on the table. Reaching for a flake, finally allowing my breathing to slow, I savoured the tiny shards of chocolate melting on my tongue, the hot tea mingling with molten sludge, trickling, pleasuring, calming.

More questions from the sergeant, less probing though, lumps of Cadbury's Snack capsizing in his mouth as he tried eating, drinking, talking simultaneously, his peaked hat beside him on the vacant seat.

What was I studying in college? Did I get a grant? What did my parents do for a living? Did I like the flat? Did I know anything else about Rosie that would be of interest to the Gardai? Finally, where was John, the boss now and where was he supposed to be picking us up later on?

Answering his questions easily, honestly, within reason, aware that time was flitting away, watching his reaction when he heard about John going on to Roscrea with Maeve and Vera, picking us up on Main Street at 6 o'clock.

Looking quickly at his watch, he rose, anxious to ring Roscrea Garda Station, get them to locate John, inform him about Rosie.

"Do you want to go back out selling them lines?" discouraging tone.

"Not really Sergeant," big blue eyes fixed on him.

"You stay put for the afternoon so, eat away at them bars, help yourself to more tea, I'll be back by and by."

Left alone, guilt made an unwelcome visit, whispering, I was good for nothing, no staying power, I'll bet ya young McLaughlin was fairly making money below in Roscrea, she wasn't sitting on her arse like a big softie, shovelling bars into her. Oh no! She was cuter than that. She wouldn't be sponging off people all week, bumming fags or cadging clothes. What odds, security won out, safe and warm in the station, unfamiliarity preferable to begging on a cold street, hungover, accosted by odious aule farmers in shit spattered wellies, no longer lumbered with a pungent pregnant Quasimodo in the throes of labour. I was staying put.

The canteen clock ticking away, saying it was 4 o'clock, no one bothering me, settling in, making more tea, smoking, reading the newspapers, tearing the wrapper off a Double Decker, yum, my favourite.

Israel and Egypt were shaking hands, Jimmy Carter seemed pleased; the cleanup was underway across Northern Ireland after a frenzy of IRA bombings. A picture of a middle-aged man, thin face and glasses, looked out at me smiling, Sir Richard Skyes, murdered in Holland by the IRA. Coughing, a piece of Double Decker going down wrong, another image stole my attention; a severe looking woman, set hair, waving, laughing young woman and man beside her, the caption stung "Thatcher foot in No. 10 Door," snobby Aishling's warning words rankled. The young guns peered in periodically, winking, nodding, amiable. Me nodding back, mild alarm summoned, maybe I had to leave, stop wasting their precious time.

5.35pm, the light was fading, I recognised the heavy footsteps approaching across the hall, Mahony, full regalia, marching towards me, head out following his veiny nose, lumpy arse steering.

"Right, the John fella has been located, he'll pick you up here any minute now, so you best get yourself ready, come out and wait in the hall," glad to be seeing the back of me I suppose.

John came through the door at 5.50pm, overcoat flapping, looking hassled. I stood, clutching my clipper board and the unsold cards evidence of my wasted day. Mahony intercepted for a moment having a quick word with the boss, putting him in the picture. Rosie was being discharged, false alarm, we had to collect her immediately.

The questions came hot and heavy as we pulled away from the station, driving under the arch for the last time. Maeve in the back nudging me, pulling an incredulous face, repeating "God" in a pensive quiet tone while I gave a rendition of events.

The boss seemed agitated, impatient behind the wheel, Vera silent, looking ahead listening to the testimony being given behind her, dramatic and persuasive. No, Rosie definitely wasn't faking it, she was in desperate pain, about to give birth at the side of the road. I got a terrible shock, Garda wouldn't let me back on the streets, insisted I stay in the station, it was a dreadful day overall, frightening, a nightmare.

The hospital lights were on. Inside the sliding doors in her wheelchair, different nurse helping, Rosie like a coiled spring leaping as John pulled up, limpedy-limp, frantic, opening the back door, pushing in beside Maeve, slam. "Come on te fuck outta here" her voice commanded and John driving off, bemused face of the nurse holding the empty chair.

"How are you Rosie?" feigned concern in John's voice.

"Grand now, delighted to be away from that shower of nosey bitches; you want to hear the battery of questions flung at me all fucking day, like the bloody Gestapo," humour creeping into her, pulling out the ten pack of Gold Bond, one left. I took a Carroll from Maeve, now stuck in the middle, still clutching her clipper board, lighting up, a collective sigh of relief in the back seat, feeling Maeve processing the pregnancy bombshell dropped so gracefully by Rosie.

"Well, how did you get on with the lines?" I knew the answer.

"Sold three full cards," displaying the proof, smug.

"Jesus, nice one. £30, that'll keep ya going for a while" I suddenly felt exhausted.

"What about yourself, Logue, did you sell much after you got rid of me?" Rosie's lips curling, elbowing Maeve who elbowed me.

"Naw, sold hardly anything, sure that sergeant Mahony wouldn't let me back out, kept me in the station for the rest of the day," winking across at her, pointing at the driver's seat, eyes warning her to behave.

"Oh typical of the boys in blue, they have a wicket spite at people selling lines," her voice convincing, hitting Maeve's knee, Maeve hitting mine, giddy collusion. Running out of steam, silence fell, lying back, heat circulating, cosy, reassuring. John turned on the radio, Elvis Costello's voice, raspy, definite… "And I would rather be anywhere else but here today."

The street lights came on as we drove onto South Circular, 91 in the distance, looking squalid and sordid, heart sinking as John pulled over to the kerb.

"Here we are ladies. Pity it wasn't a great day for ye Rosie and Cathy, better luck next time. Thanks Maeve, here's your money, well done."

We watched as he pulled away, red tail lights nipping through traffic at Garvey's, standing, subdued 'til Maeve spoke.

"Are yas hungry?"

"Starving," Rosie and I in unison.

"We'll go to the chipper, on me," Maeve sounded motherly.

Spirits restored a little, déjà vu ordering three fish suppers, retracing our footsteps up the stairs to Rosie's flat, knowing Maeve shared my instinct to protect our pregnant neighbour, make her feel cherished and safe.

We sat again at her kitchen table, eating off old newspapers, vinegar blotting the print, hoping the right words would flow comforting and warm.

"I wonder if you'll have a boy or a girl," Maeve sounding affectionate, excited.

"When my cousin Sarah was pregnant last year I said she would have a boy and I was right." Maeve was hoping for a response. "I bet you'll have a boy too."

Trying valiantly to cross her stumpy right leg over her left knee and failing Rosie turned her heavy body towards us. We smiled, waiting.

"Do you know what I'm going to tell ye lads, I couldn't give a fuck if I had a cat."

Sunday evening Ethna sat on the grubby pink sofa, pleasantly sated from her weekend in Blackrock, green eyes unblinking as Maeve and I competed, outdoing each other in announcing Rosie's pregnancy, me taking ownership of the narrative, describing events as they unfolded in Portlaoise, Maeve allowing my higher ranking in the drama.

The 16 bus to Drumcondra the following morning seemed to go purposely slow, frustrating my urgency to fill college with the news of Rosie's impregnation. The campaign began in the foyer before our first lecture, spread through the canteen at coffee break, through room 6 before lunch and back to the canteen as Betty shovelled shepherds pie onto plates whistling as I delivered the punch line "And de you know what she said, Betty... I couldn't give a fuck if I had a cat."

Even Ethna got carried away on the river of drama, finishing off sentences for me as I became breathless, or repeated sections of the story to those on the edge of the crowd gathered around me, unable to hear the details in all their gory.

By Wednesday fourth years were stopping me in the corridors, surrounding me in the foyer, asking if the story was true, their shocked gasps diluted with shrieks of mirth and delight. By Friday I was hoarse, almost unable to reply when posh Elaine took me by surprise in the canteen at afternoon coffee.

"You know Cathy I was telling mum about your friend, Rosie, and she would like to send in a gift for her."

"Yeah, my mum would like to do the same" snobby Aishling looked sincere.

Other heads were nodding, generosity was sprouting wings. Ethna and I were quiet on the bus home that evening, moved by our classmates desire to help, filled with a warmth that was alien to both of us.

There were raised voices coming from Rosie's flat and we stood in the hall, voyeurs, 'til Maeve opened No. 1's door, waving us in wide-eyed, open mouthed.

"Grainne's upstairs and she has a priest with her," Maeve trying not to smirk.

"They sound like they're arguing" Ethna was really asking a question. "You should hear the craic," Maeve was rubbing her hands in customary glee. Rod was singing too loudly "You've got me in a balltrap…" I made a scraping sound lifting the needle off to hear what Maeve was saying.

"The priest was telling her she would have to have the baby adopted and Grainne was shouting the same thing at her. Rosie shouted back that no fucking way was she having it adopted. Then the priest said she needed to see a psychiatrist, he knew a good one. Rosie said she had her own psychiatrist downstairs and he could stick his up the high hole of his arse". Maeve was rolling her eyes up to heaven, delighted that Rosie thought she was a psychiatrist.

"What else?" I wanted to hear more, ignoring the little hit to Maeve's ego.

"I didn't hear any more after that 'cos you two came in."

March was almost over, still cold, as we sat around the two-bar heater, eating our beans on toast, leaving Rod off, listening for further developments upstairs or in the hall.

Around 10 o'clock there was a commotion, shuffling sounds, a man's voice gently encouraging; "That's it, you are doing well, just one more step." Our doorbell rang; we jumped up to find Grainne moving towards the front door, Rosie between her and the priest, being oxtered along.

"She's definitely in labour this time," urgency in Grainne's voice, "her waters broke."

Rosie's head was down; her black brogues squelched a little as she limped slowly through the front door, the black skirt dipped hanging creased and damp beneath the jaded leather jacket.

"Which hospital?" Ethna's voice echoed in the hall.

"Coombe..." the front door slammed shut.

We returned to the heater, pensive, lighting up, inhaling, the noise of traffic muted in the background, something tickled my funny bone.

"Jesus, I wouldn't like to be the poor nurses delivering that baby," Maeve and Ethna looked at me expectantly.

"They'll need clothes pegs before they do anything."

"For what?" Ethna frowning.

"For their noses."

"Ya wee bitch Logue," but Maeve's shoulders were dancing.

"They'll have to use some kind of special instruments to cut her out of that jumper and skirt," Ethna was infected.

"They'll have to incinerate them," Maeve.

"Who'll carry them to the incinerator?" Ethna, eyes popping.

"They'll walk to it themselves," me snorting.

"Run you mean," now we were howling.

"We'll have another fag to wish her luck," Maeve opened a ten pack of Carrolls, "put Rod back on there Ethna."

We lay back listening to Pretty Flamingo, lost in our private fantasies, all wanting to be that girl who brightened up every boy's day. Finishing our cigarettes the beat changed, Rod was rocking it out "Took a long, long, trip to the city…"

"Come on McLaughlin, jive," I held out my hand.

"You go round."

Ethna watched us, moving in time, Maeve's arm firm, me spinning, trying to avoid the furniture, footwork rhythmic, precise.

"We'll just dance ordinary now" I pulled Ethna out of the pink armchair as Wild Side of Life began. Maeve did her Kate Bush routine while I shook my hips and head fiercely, hair flying in all directions, pretending not to notice Ethna's stilted movements, the gammy way she held her mouth half open as she shifted position between us, three dervishes whirling, beginning to feel silly, flopping heavily back into our seats as the melancholy saxophone issued the final track. The mood changed, quiet again, the lyrics of Trade Winds spoiling our mirth.

By half eleven Maeve and Ethna were asleep, I could tell by Maeve's comfortable, even breathing, Ethna's snores. Trying to feel easeful, still battling the nasty little symptoms refusing to leave me I thought about Rosie, in the throes of labour perhaps and wondered which one of her grisly, nocturnal callers was father to her child, I doubt if she knew herself.

We woke late Saturday morning, still thinking about Rosie, lying on a while chatting, sitting up in bed smoking, aware of the sun creeping in through the filthy netted curtain.

"Right, boiled eggs and toast all round?"

I loved when Maeve did that, creating a warm, homely feeling, pulling on her kimono-style dressing gown, heading for the kitchen. Ethna and I stayed put for a few more minutes until we heard the front door slam, then an urgent rapping at our flat. I got there first, opening the door to reveal Grainne, flushed and breathless, leaning on the jamb as she spoke.

"Rosie had the baby early this morning, a boy, 8lbs, 9oz."

"Ah Jesus, that's great," the three of us, in unison, urging her to come in.

"No thanks lads, I'm in a hurry, sure I'll see ye later. Visiting time is half six to half eight, no name picked yet."

She flew upstairs to Rosie's hovel; ten minutes later we heard the front door slamming as we tucked into our runny eggs, dipping soldiers of toast, all silently thinking of a name for the new arrival.

"Will we head up to the Coombe this evening?" I was boiling the kettle for the dishes.

"We might as well," Ethna sounded resigned, "sure we can walk up from here."

Maeve reminded us that her friend Mary was having a party and we were all invited; "Her flat's only a few minutes away on Harrington Street, there's a crowd of boys from U.C.D. going."

"Are any of them nice looking?" always my main concern.

"I don't know, I'm too used to looking at them every day." Maeve seemed disinterested.

"Well they couldn't be any worse than Willie or Emmet, right Ethna?" She smiled, nodding her head but her thoughts were still with Rosie.

"Sure lads we can go up to see Rosie and go on to the party then," Ethna liked her plan.

Maeve qualified, "No, we'll go up to the Coombe and then we'll go down Harcourt Street to the hotel, that's where most of them are meeting before the party."

"OK, sounds good." I was happy; at least we were walking in wide open spaces, the girls would be right there with me, no claustrophobia, no loneliness, no anticipatory fear.

"Will ye come down to the Dandelion with me, I might get something for the party," Ethna, flush as usual.

It was the last day of March, there was heat in the sun as we strolled down South Circular, creating a kind of bitter-sweet hope; maybe this would be a great day or maybe it would be typically disappointing. The market stalls were busy, though some of our old favourites were absent, their spaces filled instead with benches displaying new merchandise, colourful t-shirts, badges and posters of bands we didn't recognise or care about knowing. There were some familiar faces behind second-hand rails, chatting easily as we inspected their wares, finding nothing, the usual characters asking us for cigarettes, and being refused unless the guy was gorgeous, then we all reached into our bags hoping we might be chatted up in the process.

The omnipresent dealer, stocky in his trademark long coat, poppy eyes, wide nostrils, wondered if we needed any dope, causing Ethna and I to cower behind Maeve who remained unflapped, declining his offer, holding his gaze with her sultry brown eyes. His eyes so penetrating suddenly seemed kind as he pulled 50p from his pocket, handing it to me, without a word he walked away leaving us mystified, grateful. We laughed, wondering why he did it and what we would buy with the windfall, Ethna's suggestion made sense.

"We'll get twenty Gold Bond for Rosie."

"Good idea," Maeve reassuring, "we can't go in with one hand as long as the other."

I agreed, banishing the thought of buying silver mesh earrings, I'd ask Maeve for a lend later, she had no want of hoops and colourful danglers, I might even ask Ethna for her green cords with the gallouses, especially if she bought something new to wear.

We wandered down Grafton Street, newly paved and traffic free, following Ethna into Switzers and Arnotts hoping to spot something affordable on a sale rack. We almost expected to see Rosie with her clipper board, laughing at what she might say about the new red street that no taxi would ever drive down again. The sun kept shining; we stopped to listen to a busker outside Woolworth's singing After the Goldrush; Maeve nudging me to have a look at Ethna's face, a picture of discontent. Annoyed she hadn't purchased a new outfit, I suggested we try the boutique on Camden Street, it was on our way home and she might be lucky even though their gypsy dresses were more Maeve's style.

An Aladdin's cave of delicious colours and fabrics, I wanted so many things in there, barely hiding my envy when Ethna tried on a purple satin cat suit that fitted her perfectly, emphasising her slim frame and the blonde highlights in her hair. She beamed as we walked back up Sough Circular, nodding easily when I asked for the green cords, offering her flowery shirt too, no bother.

"Put on Rod there, Logue" Maeve opened back the double doors to the bedroom so he could serenade us while we got dressed.

"Which album, Foot Loose?"

"A Night on the Town," it's happier, Maeve was in great form.

Already in her purple cat suit Ethna slipped into a pair of black high heels saying she didn't care if they pinched her feet, looking at herself in the full-length mirror on her wardrobe door. Singing along with Rod "Tonight's the night, it's gonna be alright..." I realised I was bordering on happiness, was it possible that the nasty evil symptoms were abating slightly, don't think about it, they might gang up on me and bring a few new friends for badness.

We traded compliments, Ethna declaring that the cords suited me better, me confirming that no matter how often Maeve wore the mauve kaftan and flared jeans she always looked amazing.A final slick of lip-gloss and we were out the door, heading into unknown territory, past Dolphin's Barn down to the Coombe Maternity Hospital.

At first glance we couldn't see Rosie in the long, noisy, public ward filled with visitors, then suddenly she was there in bed number three, amused and chuckling as we walked towards her.

"Jesus, yis are a sight for sore eyes."

"Hi Rosie, congratulations" we echoed each other.

She looked drawn, tired, blue under the eyes but the devilment danced in her face, incongruous in a frilly pink nightdress, the ubiquitous red polo neck and black skirt nowhere in sight.

"Sit down will ye, you're making the place look untidy." She patted the bed and we sat, Ethna kicking off the high shoes for the time being.

"Well, ya didn't have a cat anyway," I broke the unease, all of us giggling.

"No, but he was a big bruiser, nearly killed me coming out!"

We looked around the ward, there were eight beds all surrounded by visitors, all except for Rosie's included the doting dads armed with bunches of flowers, boxes of chocolates, holding their wives' hands, beaming with pride as they talked and laughed easefully with friends and relatives.

Rosie's observant eye had already summed them up bed by bed, each inmate's idiosyncrasies documented, mimicked, nicknamed.

"Watch this performance lads, bed six, "goosy-goo" herself and yer man with the After Eights." In the bed was a pale-faced woman with a remarkably long nose, wearing rimless spectacles, the image of Mother Goose. Her husband was peeling wrappers off each square of After Eights, handing them to her with exaggerated devotion, while she took each offering, putting them in her mouth and sucking sensuously as he watched her enthralled.

"Jesus do ye see them, fucking tools," Rosie's mouth twisted.

"Look at Bill 'n' Ben up in the corner lads, watch this performance."

We obeyed, sneaking glances at the young couple in the top left-hand corner by the window who looked remarkably alike for husband and wife. Both small and dumpy with curly black hair, gesticulating wildly as they conversed, at times making slurred, garbled noises. It seemed cruel to laugh as they signed to one another but Rosie persisted pointing out the potted sunflowers he had brought her, yellow and beaming on the window sill.

"They must of run outta roses in his neck of the woods," belly jiggled, still big despite having had the baby.

Intent on continuing her commentary a cloud suddenly descended as a tall, distinguished man in a white coat peered briefly into the ward, then went on his way.

"Did ye see that fucker?" Rosie's face was closed, serious.

"Who was he?" we were intrigued.

"That's Wiggles, the head man, he's lucky I didn't put him through that door," our eyes followed noticing the metal casing, the thickness of the wood, imagining his silhouette imprinted in it cartoon like.

"Why do you not like him?" Maeve ventured.

"He came barging in here this morning, stood at the foot of me bed and says to me 'This is not your first baby is it?' The fucking cheek of him. I told him it certainly was my first baby and do you know what he said?" We shook our heads. "He said 'I believe you are lying. It was quite apparent during delivery that this wasn't your first pregnancy.' I rose meself up in the bed and I said if he didn't get the fuck outta me sight I would put him through that door."

"Did he leave ya alone then?" I was indignant.

"He did, and he better not come back near me if he knows what's good for him."

At 8 o'clock the babies were brought into their mothers from the nursery to be fed and cuddled before being put down for the night. We cooed over Rosie's boy, a big strapping baby with well defined features and a fine mop of dark hair. His mouth resembled Rosie's, with full bee-stung lips, pink and moist, wanting to be fed; the nurse handed Rosie his bottle.

Ethna asked what was she going to call him.

"I'm thinking Mark Anthony."

Instantly the same phrase came to all our minds; 'Friends, Romans, Countrymen, lend me your ears!' We tried damage limitation. "Mark is lovely, but Anthony is so common, would you not consider something different as his second name" I reasoned.

Maeve helped "Yeh, something like Adam or Karl."

Ethna seemed more interested in putting on her black high heels, a signal that it was time to go. She handed Rosie the twenty Gold Bond, promising that we'd be back to see her Monday evening.

Darkness was creeping in, the street lights were coming on as we walked quickly back down South Circular, past Kelly's Corner, heading to Harcourt Street, sweet anticipation flowing as we reached the hotel, the sound of traditional music, loud raucuos voices reaching the street. Mary and the party-goers had taken over a large corner of the lounge, chatting, laughing noisily, their tables covered with drinks. Maeve got in the first round while Ethna and I surveyed the talent, surely to God U.C.D. would offer up some decent looking bucks having a larger gene pool to work with than our incestuous excuse for a college. I only needed one hunk to make the night exciting and there he was chatting to Maeve at the bar, tall, long blonde hair in a ponytail, checked shirt and jeans, definitely my cup of tea.

"Who was that fella at the bar?" I tried to keep calm.

"That's Owen, he's a cousin of Mary's from Galway, he's up for the weekend."

"How do you know him?" I wondered if she fancied him.

"He comes up a lot, stays with Mary, I met him a good few times over the years" her voice gave nothing away.

"He's a nice piece of stuff," I tested the water.

"Do you think? I'll get you talking to him in a while."

Great, so Maeve didn't fancy him; I took my glass of Smithwicks from her, grateful, relieved she wasn't going to be my competition this time.

By 11pm we were relaxed, merry, walking up Harrington Street, following the crowd, all carrying brown paper bags, Owen and his friends behind us singing 'Stairway to Heaven' in shouty, out of tune voices. Mary's flat was party ready with furniture pushed back in the sitting room to create a dance floor, plates of nibbles on a table against the wall, some extra beers, cheap wine on a sideboard in the kitchen. We held on to our six packs tightly, reluctant to leave them with the communal stash lest they be consumed by the usual parasites who arrived to parties, uninvited, empty handed.

The red paper lampshade created the right atmosphere as the music started and the first four amazing notes rang out, then repeated, urging us to dance but we stood waiting for the drum call, then the low pulsating bass… "I been driving all night, my hands wet on the wheel…" was all we needed. Beers shoved under seats we freed our hands, shaking our heads, shoulders, hips, we let it fly. The next few songs were mixed, some singles, some album tracks. I pouted in Owen's direction, trying to move like Debbie Harry as Heart of Glass played, Maeve channelling Kate Bush, Ethna doing her best not to look too dorky, keeping her moves small and safe. We drank when the songs didn't suit us, moving subtly towards Owen's corner. Gloria Gaynor promising she would survive, Maeve finally asking him had he met Ethna and I before, me giving him my killer-sexy-eyed look. We danced together to Bob Seger's 'Hollywood Nights' and track after track 'til he finally took hold of me as the tempo slowed and Bob sang "We've got tonight, who needs tomorrow…" Both drunk, he leaned heavily on me, smell of sweat in his hair, now hanging loose on his shoulders, asking me the same question over and over, wet mouth against my ear.

"Do you want to come upstairs to bed?"

"Sure we're time enough, let's dance for another while."

"Oh come on, I'm fed up dancing, I want to make love," he slurred in a soft Galway accent but his body felt hard against me.

"It's too risky," I felt stupid, childish.

"OK, we can just do a sixty niner, no worries there."

"Right, well I'll just go and tell the girls, be back in a minute," smiling, radiating calm, trying not to run across the room to where Maeve and Ethna stood chatting to a group of girls I didn't recognise. I tugged at the sleeve of Maeve's kaftan; she saw the look on my face.

"What's up with you?" her eyes narrowed.

"What is a sixty-nine, what the fuck is a sixty-nine? That's what yer man wants me to do with him."

"Come out to the toilet with me and I'll tell you" she pushed me gently, steering me in to the empty bathroom, locking the door.

I listened, eyebrows rising higher, mouth moving as though I were sucking on a bitter sherbet.

"Yuck, no fucking way am I doing that, how will I get out of this, he'll think I'm a big baby."

"Just stay over beside us for a while, we're gonna have a singsong now anyway; he'll be too drunk in a while to know what he's at."

Reassured; we returned to the sitting room as Mary invited us all to sit anywhere, chairs, floor, people were going to sing. A small dark-haired man was tuning his guitar and someone shouted "Suzanne" and we clapped and cheered as he began singing, helping with the chorus, relieved that he knew all the lyrics.

The group of girls Maeve had been talking to earlier volunteered their friend Frances to sing next and she stood up, poised, confident, telling the guitar man the song was in A. She launched into 'You've Got a Friend' but she had a thin little voice with no power, no soul. I knew I wanted to sing next, aware of the stabbing butterflies in my tummy, the dryness in my mouth that I tried to banish with a slug of beer.

"Right, Cathy next for a song," Maeve's voice was loud, Ethna watching with protective eyes.

I stood up, if yer wan could do it so could I. Guitar man asked what key my song was in but I waved my hand saying I would sing unaccompanied, announcing that I wanted everyone to click their fingers and provide the beat. I led the way, clicking as I sang "My analyst told me that I was right out of my head, the way he described it…." I sounded good, people were smiling, clicking, one or two jazz enthusiasts making the right noises, then I hit a wall. "They all laughed… blank. I tried again, "they all laughed at… blank. The clicking stopped, one more go; "they all laughed at…" A sandy haired girl, slightly plump, sitting with the Frances wan and a few others looked disgusted "Sit down, give someone else a chance," sniggering, dismissive. Ethna suddenly looked scared. Maeve tugged lightly at my greed corduroys.

"Listen FATTY!" I spat "butt out."

"Right Mrs. Farmer with your gallouses!" more sniggering.

"Yeah right, FAT ARSE."

There were shrieks of ooh! from fatty's corner as Maeve tugged harder at my trousers, Ethna saying "Don't mind her Cathy, sit down, you can sing another one in a while."

I took her advice, my anger forgotten about instantly amid another slurred, shouty version of Stairway to Heaven from Owen and company, poor guitar man floundering as they changed from key to key shamelessly. Although Maeve patted my knee I realised I wasn't annoyed, opening my last bottle, I raised it towards Fatty, winking cheers at her and she raised her bottle winking her reply.

It was 3am, the singing fizzled out, no one could remember lyrics, guitar man snapped his guitar case closed, some revellers were asleep, open mouthed, Owen snoring loudly in the corner, thank God.

"Will we head, lads?" Ethna sounded tired.

We thanked Mary for the invites, found our jackets creased and crumpled under the sofa and headed into the hall lighting our consoling cigarettes, grateful we hadn't far to walk in the chilly night air.

The last to sleep as usual, I lay waiting for invisible fingers tightening around my neck, pins and needles surging, a racing, pounding heart, they didn't appear. The pillow, no longer a boulder caressed, my head, limbs melted oozing into the mattress, legs akimbo. Sleep whispered to me and I relented to her charm.

We went into college early Monday morning, taking the 8 o'clock bus across town, paying the correct fare; Ethna and I equally excited to announce the good news.

Glad tidings spread through the smoke-filled foyer. Reluctant to go to Brennan's lecture we watched the clock as he warbled on about Wordsworth's Lucy poems.

Posh Elaine and Snobby Aishling arrived late to the canteen making a beeline for our table, smiling, breathless.

"There you are Cathy, Mum sent this in for your friend, we chose lemon as we can't predict what she'll have, obviously."

Elaine placed a quilted drawstring baby bag on the table beside me decorated in yellow teddies, filled with baby bottles, teats, Milton sterilising fluid, newborn nappies, all the necessary paraphernalia. Aishling followed suit handing me a gift bag, telling me to look at the contents, see what I thought.

I held up the tiny white babygros, brushed my cheek against the soft fluffy blanket, swallowing down the lump in my throat, ignoring the tears threatening to spill out of Ethna's eyes, my voice came out funny and small.

"Thanks a million girls, she had a boy you know, yeah, Saturday morning, 8lbs 9oz, he's gorgeous, yeah."

They seemed genuinely delighted, wondering if there was anything else they could do, looking in their purses for change, eager to phone their mothers with the news.

Left alone at the table Sr. Marie Claire joined me, her kind open face listening closely, drawing me out, asking how I was, displaying little interest in Rosie's story.

Disarmed, I heard myself telling her about my nightmare in the cinema, the hellish symptoms since, the fear that I was losing my mind.

"Do you know, Cathy dear, there's a counselling service here on the grounds, in the prefab. by the front gate, why don't we go down now and make an appointment, it's free for students of the college," no judgement in her voice. We walked together, carrying Rosie's gifts, Marie Claire waiting outside in April sun while I talked to the secretary, getting an appointment for Friday, 3 o'clock.

In the Coombe that evening Rosie seemed subdued, quiet, no name-calling, no mimicking, no belly wobbling with mirth or devilment. She accepted the gifts without comment, putting them in her locker while we overcompensated describing the frenzy her news caused in college, suggesting new baby names, trying to make her laugh, wondering did she knock aule Wiggles into the middle of next week.

"I'm calling him Mark Anthony" – no trace of humour in her voice.

Silenced, recovering quickly we agreed that it was a good strong name, classic really.

Wednesday evening our doorbell went, there stood Rosie in a blue floral dress, cream cardigan, her sleeping boy in her arms, Grainne standing behind her.

"Come in, come in," whispering our excitement, lifting books off her favourite pink chair, putting a frayed cushion behind her as she sat, thrilled to see her navy patent shoes, her smoky grey tights. Grainne hovered, refusing to sit, they were in a hurry she said, Fr. Dessie was outside in the car, giving them a lift to Clondalkin, Rosie was staying with her for a while. "Right, well we're away home for Easter on Wednesday but we'll be back on the 22nd ready for babysitting duties," I laughed, winking at her, Rosie winked back. Maeve helping her out of the chair, baby still sound asleep. They were gone, leaving a hollow empty feeling in the room that Rod couldn't displace with Hot Legs and we switched on the heater, inhaling our cigarettes, exhaling slowly, silent, pensive.

Friday 3.15pm I sat in the reception area of the Counselling Unit, the secretary smiling kindly from behind her desk, telling me they were running a little behind but I shouldn't be waiting too much longer. Five minutes later a tall, grey haired man, looked around dad's age, invited me into his office, offering me a seat, a small coffee table between us, glass of water for me to drink. His voice was warm, reminding me that a problem shared was a problem halved, encouraging, nodding his head thoughtfully while I relayed the cinema story, describing the nasty symptoms, admitting that they weren't as acute of late. We talked, over and back for an hour, relief that my childhood was not mentioned, no empty clichés, his final reassuring words struck home beautifully. I had a panic attack, yes, my mind had betrayed me, so I lived in fear, in a constant state of flight or fight manifested in unpleasant physical symptoms such as pins and needles, tightening in my throat and head, disturbed sleep patterns. However; now the ultimate redemptive statement: I was not going mad, not at all, I was entirely sane, normal.

Thanking him, shaking his hand, walking into an April shower, smiling, up the driveway to college, a lightness surging through me, sun beaming through the rain; Ethna would be in the canteen, so would Marie Claire, dying to see their lovely faces.

The landlord was around early Saturday morning, pounding on doors, looking for rents, Maeve had already gone home for Easter, leaving her keys behind in case Rosie wanted to use the flat in our absence. It was marginally more comfortable than her own sty.

Ethna and I trawled Henry Street for the afternoon, sick of our drab winter clothes, needing something new for the holidays, determined, watching each other, silent competition, both wanting to win. Gaywear sent us into a spin, lusting after everything in the store, ages in the trying on rooms, deciding, advising, money foremost in my mind, mum's warning voice in my head. Ethna had no such worry, casually choosing white straight legged cotton jeans, a white cotton jumper with flowers embroidered in wool on the front, finishing off with a navy blazer, sorted. For weeks I had stopped overeating, back smoking, my appetite decreased as did my weight, beaming now at the slim girl in the mirror wearing a calf-length floral smocked dress in blues and reds, complete with long sleeves, it would be perfect with cowboy boots. My hair had grown to shoulder length, my blue eyes seemed bigger, brighter, Jesus I was beginning to look like Joni Mitchell. My hand shook writing the cheque, it wasn't fear or guilt but more delicious excitement, satisfaction bordering on joy, not caring about mum's cross-examination, she'd just have to get over it.

Ethna beamed too, almost smug we walked towards O'Connell Street both thinking the same thought.

"We'll go to Pizzaland Logue, I'll pay."

"Let's have a carafe of wine to celebrate our new duds, I'll get that."

We lingered over the food, savouring every bite of thin crispy pizza, sipping pale red wine slowly, lighting our cigarettes as the waitress cleared plates and we resisted ordering deep baked apple pie with cream.

The evening sun held a promise of summer as we sauntered along Dame Street, turning on to South Great George's Street carrying our precious purchases, the pavements getting less crowded as we reached Camden Street, promising to help each other put together some nice outfits for Easter when we reached 91 South Circular.

Rosie surprised us with a visit Sunday afternoon, limpedy-limping to her throne, still wearing her fragrant floral dress, offering us a Gold Bond, we declined, lighting our Carrolls wondering how Mark Anthony was, when was she returning to her hovel.

"I left him in Grainne's, her husband gave me a lift over, I just had to get a few things, check the post, he'll be back for me in an hour, it's good to get away from the bloody screeching for a while lads," she sighed heavily, exhaling pale blue smoke into the room.

"When will you be back?" Maeve told me to ask her that.

"I'll be back this weekend, Grainne's on me fucking case the whole time and that humpy bollocks of a Fr. Dessie has me bloody mithered preaching, he's from home but he's a nosey aule poof" she smirked, a flash of devilment showing in her eyes.

"Well listen Rosie, we'll be away 'til Saturday week so you're welcome to stay here with the baby, it's a wee bit more comfortable than your place," I handed her Maeve's keys. She dropped them into the Dunnes plastic carrier bag on the floor beside her, saying she probably wouldn't use them but thanks anyway. The doorbell rang as she threw her cigarette butt into the empty grate, rising without too much effort from the pink armchair, limpedy-limp up the corridor shouting "See yas!" the front door slamming behind her.

"She looks good," Ethna's eyes widened.

"It wouldn't be hard, wonder what she did with the black skirt and the red polo-neck?"

I really wanted to know.

"Sure they were only fit to be burned," Ethna looked disgusted.

"Suppose that dress'll be on her for a few years now," I was starting to feel giddy.

"The tights will get destroyed and won't be replaced," Ethna was sniggering.

"Her legs'll turn blue as the winter sets in, to match the dress," both sniggering now.

We stayed on that trail for a while, painting a picture of Rosie in a new navy leather coat, matching her shoes, resplendent outside Switzers with her clipper board 'til the realisation that she was a mother sobered us up, raising new questions.

"I wonder does she have a crib for Mark Anthony?" practical Ethna.

"She never said. She didn't say anything nice either about the lovely things we got her in college, Jesus that stuff was expensive," I was beginning to feel disappointment for Snobby Aishling and Posh Elaine.

"I'd say compliments don't come easy to her" Ethna made sense, "we'll tell Aishling and Elaine that she loved everything and couldn't get over their kindness."

"Yeah, you're right, Ethna, that's what we'll do. I hope we see her using the stuff though, it would be a wild waste otherwise."

"Sure you know we'll see her using it, we're bound to."

We headed home for Easter, class of '78. The announcement of summer exams ringing in our ears. Father Weller had drawn our attention to the timetables going up in the front hall Wednesday morning, we jostled around the notice board informing us, May 21st to 25th, a week of exams then home for the summer.

Ethna filled a large suitcase with winter clothes taking them home now lightening her load for the journey in late May. Lazy, not wanting to be weighed down on the bus I travelled with rucksack only placing it carefully in the overhead compartment, lighting up a cigarette, delighted no one sat beside me, relaxed, at ease.

The parish was jam-packed with visitors out from the North in their caravans and holiday homes, driving big boxy Volvos and sleek Mercedes Benzes. We stood at the back of the crammed chapel Sunday morning, Malachy and I nursing hangovers, hoping mum would produce an aule bottle of Nicholas with the leg of lamb after mass. We didn't listen to a word the priest said, nipping out for a cigarette at communion, we'd have to dodge mum's questions about the sermon and what the notices were when we got home. The Sinn Fein boys were selling Easter lilies for our lapels at the chapel gate. Maeve and I spent the week drinking, flirting with posh, protestant boys from Belfast and not so posh boys from the Bogside who made us laugh with jokes about the Queen, outdoing each other with swaggering tales of defiance against British soldiers and the R.U.C. Flattered by attention from posh boys, I lied through my smiles, sipping crème de menthe frappes, mimicking their clipped accents talking about 'Mummy's B.M.W.' or 'Daddy's buying me a wee place in Dublin while I attend Trinity, och just got a wee pad on Fitzwilliam Square." They fell for it like gormless twits asking for my phone number, offering to take me home in their daddy's car, me declining the latter knowing the myth would be shattered if they stepped inside my faded, rundown home.

Mum was in good form though, dad's work managing the local hotel hampered his binges, keeping him out of harm's way, putting a smile on her face with a healthy bank balance. The clouds of tension dissipated slightly, sitting in the back garden watching mum knitting, the warm April sun seeping into our bones, turning my skin light brown, first time ever. First time too I balked at the thought of going back to college and exams and most of all 91 South Circular. The thought of Mark Anthony cheered me a little.

Sunday 22nd the express bus pulled out of Letterkenny at 4 o'clock, my last time heading back as a first year, maybe Maeve's last time ever.

"I am not looking forward to these stupid summer exams," offering Maeve a cigarette.

"First year exams are a doddle. Hopefully I'll get a 1.1 in my degree, be heading to the States in October" she sounded confident.

"You have an uncle out there in California, don't ya?" I remembered he was damn handsome too.

"Aye, Gordon, I'm going out to him for the summer anyway, whether I get the 1.1 or not. Have you any plans?" she yawned, knowing the answer would be boring.

"Dad has a job lined up for me in the hotel working upstairs; I'll be staying in the staff quarters that should be a bit of craic." I was excited at the prospect.

We fell asleep after Monaghan, not waking 'til we pulled in at Bus Aras, brightness reminding me that summer was within reach as we pulled on our rucksacks heading to O'Connell Street for the no. 16. Ethna opened the flat door before Maeve had a chance to turn the key, her face pale, urgent, ushering us inside with a wave of her arm, her mouth moving but no words sounding.

"What's up?" Maeve laughed softly.

I expected to see Rosie inside with her sleeping boy and moved on my tiptoes.

"Someone robbed us lads, our stuff is gone," shocked tone.

We looked around the sitting room, slowly, silently, feeling the sparsity, the naked spots, the empty ledges and corners. Bare mantelpiece, no camera, no tape-recorder, no candlesticks. Little corner table sad, record player gone along with our two precious albums, no more Rod. Shivering, moving towards the bedroom Ethna watching our faces knowing already what lay ahead. No love beads, dangling earrings, birthday gifts, rings or bracelets or parker pens in fancy boxes. Back towards the sitting room the cruellest blow of all, no two-bar heater.

"The fucking bitch, the fucking limpedy bitch," I was shouting.

The penny dropped in Maeve's dark brown eyes.

"Do ya think it was her?" almost a whisper.

Ethna rushed past us, out the open door, up the stairs to Rosie's hovel; we stood in silence, waiting, rucksacks on the floor between us.

"She's gone. Her flat is wide open, so is her bedroom, nothing left but the smell lads." Ethna, incredulous, angry too. We stood with Maeve in the hall, her long slim index finger dialling 999, her voice explaining that we had been burgled, her head nodding saying "Right... right... OK then."

"They'll send someone round in the morning, too busy now," she hung up the receiver.

We unpacked our clean clothes sighing loudly in turn, weary and heavy of heart. As always Ethna had food from home, meat, apple tart, home-made bread.

"I'll put this in the fridge, make us a cup of tea," already in her pyjamas.

"Ah no lads, I don't fucking believe it."

"What?" Maeve and I together, running to the kitchen.

"She even took the bloody kettle."

We slept fitfully, all up and dressed by 8 o'clock Monday morning ready for the doorbell which rang loudly at 9.15am. In stepped Detective John Connelly, plainclothes, matter of fact, taking a few notes in his little notebook, walking around the flat behind us, listening, nodding.

"Have you any idea who might have done this girls?" he raised his eyebrows, watching our faces.

"We think it was our neighbour who lived upstairs," Maeve assigning herself leader. "I gave her my key before Easter, told her she could stay here if she wanted."

The can of worms was wide open, the questions came hard and heavy. The story tumbled out, each of us interjecting, painting a picture for him, Rosie, her hovel, clipper board, Switzers, pregnancy, birth and now, gone with our stuff. The tale unfolded and his eyes drifted off in the distance filling with recognition, resignation, sitting on the edge of the frayed sofa, he shook his head, pursing his lips, sighing sadly.

"Does this Rosie walk with a limp?"

Staring at him the ground seemed to shift, how did he know that?

"Her real name is Rosemary Flynn" he motioned us to sit down, she's from Tipperary, not Limerick, she's a real piece of work."

Entranced we listened, a new portrait of Rosie revealing itself so different to our rambunctious, warm, funny companion. The truth and the lies were separated, ironed out, leaving no doubt. Yes, she was from a big family, the third of ten, born with a limp into an impoverished farming background, left home at 16, never looked back. Known to the Gardaí for quite a while, 26 years old, had lived in various hovels around South Dublin since arriving here ten years ago. "Always on the game if you know what I mean!"

He stood up putting pen and notebook in his jacket pocket.

"We'll do our best to find her, girls," he sounded sympathetic, "but your stuff will be well gone by now."

We sat watching as he moved towards the door, his hand on the latch, he turned towards us.

"By the way this is not her first child, she's had two other babies that we're aware of, adopted. Right, well I'll be in touch."

We headed into college, Ethna and I getting our stories straight on the 16A, Rosie the legend would live on in the minds of every student who had taken her to their hearts. Posh Elaine, Snobby Aishling would be charmed to hear that the social workers had found a cute little flat for herself and Mark Anthony to start a new life in, yeah, just around the corner from us. She would get the unmarried mother's allowance, no more hawking lines on Grafton Street or any other street for that matter. She could live a nice peaceful life, rearing her baby boy, using all the lovely gifts she received from everyone, she was so grateful. There would be no sneering faces to be endured from Joey or Emmet, Willie could still smile away like a buffoon and lick his teeth twenty licks a minute, with delight. Betty in the canteen would throw admiring glances at us, heaping our plates with extra victuals, clap our backs in McGowan's with a few whiskeys in her and tell us we were grand women helping out a poor girl like Rosie.

The library was packed in the afternoons, cramming for exams, supplying missed lecture notes, swapping reading material, forming study groups where we could pick geeks' brains on the difference between macro and microevolution. We took smoking breaks, sitting in the foyer talking, laughing, singing the odd song if Oisín was there with his guitar. Sr. Marie Claire would find me from time to time, wondering how I was, pat my hand affectionately, satisfied I was recovering. Fr. Weller passed through now and again, going to his office upstairs, bobbing his head smiling, sanctioining.

The flat was quiet without Rod. We boiled water for tea in a saucepan, sitting around, rudderless without our heater even though summer had arrived bringing warm temperatures we still felt the chill of the evenings in our cavernous sitting room. Mr. Tommy Heenan refused to claim compensation for our lost belongings on his house insurance saying it was our own fault for providing the thief with a key, no insurance company would pay out under such circumstances, the prick. After May came we avoided being in when he called for his rent, lurking in Mary's flat on Harrington Street Saturday mornings 'til we knew he was gone. Ethna spent every weekend in Blackrock with her cousin detesting the flat, using it only as a place to sleep. Maeve and I inveigled ourselves into other people's flats, people from secondary school who under normal circumstances we wouldn't be seen dead with but they had food and fires and best of all, televisions. Sometimes we brought six packs and crisps, making the best of it.

After two weeks waiting to hear from Detective Connelly, we forgot all about him only to be surprised when he called one Friday evening, May 4th with news of Rosie.

"We located her girls," no triumph in his voice, "she's working as a domestic in Baggot St. Hospital. She denied all knowledge of the theft, even came with us gladly in the squad car to her flat in Ranelagh so we could search it." A tiny grin was forming at the sides of his mouth. "She refused to come in with us though, sat in the car smoking, saying she wished us luck and hoped we would find everything. She is some detail." Of course they found nothing and there was no more to be done or said except 'Goodbye detective' and 'Thanks very much!' No doubt

Ethna was wolfing down roast chicken and stuffing followed by ice-cream and jelly while Maeve and I sat smoking, staring into the empty grate.

"John Kelly's having a party tomorrow night, meeting in Slattery's first, fancy going?"

"Maeve are you mad? There is no way I am going anywhere near Rathmines or anywhere over Portabello Bridge."

"Jesus Logue, what's wrong with ya?" she was laughing.

"What if we ran into Rosie, she knows that we reported her to the Guards don't forget, Christ I would die of embarrassment."

"God you're right," she suddenly looked worried, "aye, we would look like big babies, worse still though she might be angry, Lord I hope she doesn't send a few hard men round here to put manners on us." We both looked worried then, double locking the flat door before getting into bed, talking into the small hours, making ourselves laugh with images of Rosie in Nazi uniform limpedy marching up South Circular to get to us, army of burly misfits in her wake, one uglier than the other. "Jesus, could it get any worse," I didn't mean to speak aloud but Maeve was sound asleep.

The atmosphere in 91 was different now, quiet, deserted. The girl in the top flat was rarely seen, like a ghost she came and went, footsteps on the stairs, front door opening, closing. Pat and Dominic still lived in the basement flat no. 3 with its own separate entrance, they didn't have to come through the front hall and since Rosie left they seldom did. Now and again we'd spot them heading to Garveys for pints late in the evening, still bright as we walked to the chipper hankering after spice burgers or battered sausages, bored with the beans or scrambled eggs on toast.

We managed to avoid Tommy Heenan three Saturdays in a row making Ethna nervous that it was too good to be true, warning that we would never get away with it, he was bound to call around at an unexpected time, catch us in. She was partially right. May 14th, Monday morning early, the phone rang in the hall, I answered it. "This is Mr. Heenan's secretary I'd like to speak to someone from flat no. 1."

"I'm from no. 1, Cathy Logue here."

"Miss Logue, I'm ringing on behalf of the landlord. You ladies are three weeks behind in your rent, Mr. Heenan is a busy man, he travels throughout the country during the week, Saturday is the only day he's in town, he expects you all to pay what you owe him in full when he calls this Saturday the 19th. Is that clear?"

"Is there any chance he would extend it to the 26th? We're all waiting for the last instalment of our student grants to come through, we'll definitely have the money by then" my most sincere voice.

"In that case Miss Logue make sure you all pay up and by the way Mr. Heenan checked the flat last Saturday in your absence, you will owe him £10 each on top of the arrears to cover the cost of the missing sideboard." I slammed the receiver down hard, cursing Tommy Heenan to hell.

Ethna was counting down the days and so was I, both aching to get out of Dublin for the summer, wishing we hadn't to jump that last major hurdle before West Cork and Donegal opened their arms to embrace us.

Lectures were officially over, giving us a study week before exams time to return library books, pay outstanding fees, check the lost property for belongings.

The licks haunted the library, hogging reference texts, nervous and reluctant to leave their desks in case their goodies were nabbed, we watched, hoping hunger would beckon, luring them out to the canteen. Their perseverance rarely wavered, while we fidgeted, losing concentration, reading the same line a hundred times without comprehension, comforted to see kindred spirits going for another cigarette, joining them in the foyer vowing this would be our last for at least an hour.

Harnessing brain power, we spent afternoons with other rebels and misfits, forming study groups, collating lectures, making sense of each subject, a quiet confidence growing, bringing peace, courage. New friendships were forming, bonds deepening, Ethna and I were reluctant to part company with the kindreds each evening, loath to take the 16A across town where we felt lonely and isolated in 91 South Circular. Walking out of college Friday 18th someone yelled our names running behind us, smiling and breathless.

"Listen lads, why don't ye come over and stay with us during the exams" it was Lynn from Sligo. "Come over Sunday evening, there's plenty of room in our flat, sure we can do a bit of study and have a bit of craic too."

The warm feeling was back again, sitting upstairs in the front seat of the 16A, both staring out the window, lighting up, exhaling contentedly, the bus crawling up Wexford Street in Friday evening traffic.

The trees on Harrington Street were blooming, the evening sun still potent as we moved up South Circular Road, both eager to get to Sunday, pack our rucksacks and cross town again, rejoin the kindreds and face down those exams.

The phone rang Saturday evening around 10pm, the phantom from upstairs answered it, knocking on our door announcing curtly "it's for Maeve somebody."

Cigarette suspended in mid-air she looked suspicious, hesitant.

"Go on, you better answer it, might be your mother," I sounded impatient.

"What if it's Heenan?" Maeve equally impatient, "He could be threatening to evict us."

"If it is him put me on the phone I'll soon tell him a thing or two, like we're going to report him to the Health Board about the state of that toilet," I could feel the anger rising.

Through the opened door I listened to Maeve's voice high pitched, pleasant, happy saying "Great… Yeah… lovely… that suits us… perfect… right, see ya then."

"Guess who that was?" she closed the flat door, eyes narrowed, smiling.

"Well I know it wasn't Mr. Tommy fart face," I sounded casual. Ethna just back from her cousin's in Blackrock stared "Was it your mum?"

"No me dears, it was the bould Finian, Rustic are playing in Limerick next Thursday and he's coming to

Dublin Friday, he's bringing his own car, wants to stay here Friday night."

"I'll be away home straight after the last exam, pulling out of Heuston at one o'clock," Ethna couldn't wait.

"I'm finished Thursday but I'll need Friday to pack and get organised, so it suits me grand that Finian's coming, it'll be a lift home Saturday morning," Maeve was content.

"I'll leave the rent money with ye lads before I go, £40 plus the £10 he wants for the drawers we burned." Good honest Ethna.

"Aye, that's fine, we'll pay him before we leave Saturday morning. Jesus I'm delighted to be getting a lift too, didn't fancy lugging that ole suitcase of mine down to Bus Aras," excitement was beginning to mount inside me.

We took the 16 bus across town Sunday evening for the last time, Ethna's rucksack packed to the gills, mine filled with what I needed 'til Friday, both of us happy to be joining the kindreds. Dressed in our faded jeans, cotton summer tops and Jesus sandals, the bus practically empty, sitting on the back seat upstairs, our legs crossed, resting on the opposite seat. The open windows created a breeze as the conductor made his way towards us, sweat patches in the armpits of his short sleeved, blue shirt. He lurched forward grabbing the seat in front of us, bus making a wide turn onto Dame Street.

"Fares please ladies," eyeing our freshly lit cigarettes.

"Would ya like a drag?" Ethna's voice surprised me.

He accepted her offer, pushing in between us, exhaling as he spoke good humouredly, inquiring after our destination.

"There you go loves," he stood punching out our tickets, declining the coins in our outstretched hands with a wink. "Have a nice evening ladies," he moved back down the bus, new passengers getting on in Westmorland Street, watching them embark, girls in floppy hats, Laura Ashley dresses, fresh and delicate like brightly coloured butterflies.

"That was nice of him," I nudged Ethna gently on the arm.

"At least we won't have to be jumping off if the inspector gets on Logue," returning the nudge playfully.

The warm feeling was back, a welcome visitor replacing doubt and loneliness and fear. Something beautiful was happening to me, I let myself acknowledge it. I felt normal again. No tightening sensations anywhere in my body, no pins and needles, no palpitations or heart surges or sweaty palms and absolutely no fear, thank you, thank you God.

McGowan's sounded packed, passing its open door on our way to Howard's corner shop, needing fig rolls and Mikado's, maybe some Club Milks to share over copious cups of tea as we talked, laughed, studied for the next five days.

We pooled change, Ethna throwing in an extra 50p for jellies she loved, a Bounty Bar for me, moving towards the counter passing the newspaper stand. 'The Sunday World' pulled me up short. The headline in red capitals zoomed, yelling 'Charity Cards Dumped in Dublin Mountains', a short paragraph read "A shocking discovery was made by a group of hikers on Friday morning last as they stumbled across hundreds of partially burned charity cards for autistic children dumped unceremoniously in the Dublin Mountains. Continued on pages 22/23"

Ethna beside me opening the paper finding the inside pages, photographs of pink cards, partially burned, bags and bags of them strewn across the rocky ground, cards that had been sold, signatures still visible on some, most charred, erased forever.

"Jesus Ethna, Maeve and I are in big trouble, the Gardai know we sold them cards," my heart was racing again, a hint of pins and needles.

"No, no, Cathy, look," she had continued reading pointing out the final paragraph, whispering it quickly to me, aware we were being watched from behind the counter.

"Shamefully there will be no prosecutions as the registration of charities in Ireland continues to be a grey area with most charities having to donate just 10% of earnings to their chosen cause."

"Oh Jesus, thanks be to God," my breath came back, spurting, heaving, leaning on the paper stand composing myself.

"You're alright Logue," mild amusement in Ethna's voice, eyes smiling, reassuring.

"For a minute there I thought I was a gonner, the gates of Mountjoy slammed behind me." I was starting to chuckle. We paid for our sugary goods, emerging into May sunlight again, relieved, laughing, peace restored, walking towards the kindreds' flat on Iona Road.

"Wonder if there's a phone in the girls' flat, I'd love to ring Maeve and tell her the craic."

"I wouldn't say they have a phone, it's time enough to tell her on Friday. Forget about it now."

"Aye, you're right Mullins. I wonder was it the John fella dumped them cards? Betya Rosie knew all about it. So much for the draw and the new car!"

Ethna made no reply, only opened her bumper packet of jelly beans, fishing out the green ones, happy in the knowledge that she had not fallen under Rosie's spell, not really; had probably seen right through her from the start with those suspicious, calculating, bottle green eyes.

We felt at home with the kindreds, united, moving gently through the week, swapping resources, ideas. We ate late Sunday evening, revision complete, feeling prepared for hurdle one. Ethna and I sharing a single bed, the three kindreds spooning in the double, alarm clock set, Janis Ian on the tape recorder, drifting off, 'Jessie come home, there's a hole in the bed where we slept…' and in the winter extra blankets for the cold,'Routines developed, easy rhythms, food, clothes, exams, study, food, music, sleep. The mornings brought anticipation, fake nonchalance, hysterics outside exam halls when Roscommon geek mentioned a mysterious topic that was definitely coming up or post-mortom-exam dork insisting that Nietzsche not Satre said 'God is dead!' Comforting platitudes ruled then.

"It's only a small part of the exam lads," kindred one.

"The swots don't know everything," kindred two.

"It's over now, forget about it," kindred three.

"We're bound to pass lads," Ethna.

"Sure what the fuck odds," me.

Staying three hours in the exam hall proved difficult with the sun luring us, every cough a distraction or possible code, longing for cigarettes, the first to capitulate leaving, followed by a trail of rebels who wrapped up regurgitating notes even though we could have spewed on for another while.

In the canteen at lunchtime Big Betty piled on the chips, winking encouragement, a ship in full sail, "cheer up there girleens, yeer doing well, only two more to go."

"Thanks Betty," me and Ethna moving our trays along.

"How's that friend o' yours and the new baby?"

"Oh great, Betty, she's getting on great" in unison.

"Well fair play te ye, ye looked after her so well, don't forget te pick up your ice-cream 'n' jelly there. Move along now folks."

Friday arrived, the sun warm on our faces, crossing the road above McGowan's, Ethna weighed down with the heavy rucksack, up the narrow laneway to college, ecstatic, one final hurdle to freedom. The foyer throbbed, students from every year, sharing summer plans, impatient to be gone, culchies all ready to bolt, their bags and cases piled up in the entrance hall, only snacks available in the canteen, Big Betty knew the drill. Mr Brennan stood in the doorway as we shuffled into the exam hall, trying to give him my sexiest smile, something to remember me by when he was correcting the papers. No one left early, not even the rebels, we liked English, we liked Brennan, wanted to please him, do well. He sat at the lectern peering over his black square rimmed glasses finally announcing we had ten minutes to go, biros picking up pace, the final burst at the last hurdle.

"Bye Mr. Brennan, have a nice summer" leaving my paper on his desk, a last suggestive smile, better safe than sorry.

The foyer was buzzing again, very few availing of the snacks only shouting 'goodbye' to Big Betty, heading towards the front hall, gathering up belongings, echoes of "Bye everyone… see yas… have a great summer, give me a ring won't you…. byeee…" I stood with Ethna at the bus stop on Lower Drumcondra Road, "Cathy put that in your bag the money I owe Heenan, don't lose it" she handed me five £10 notes. The 16A appearing in the distance, taking her to O'Connell Street where she'd walk down the quays a short distance to the bus stop for Heuston. South Circular was still my destination for the last time though and I watched Ethna struggle with her rucksack, waving goodbye on the pavement as we pulled away over O'Connell Bridge, I wondered if we would live together next year, just the two of us, without Maeve.

I remembered then that Maeve would be in the flat when I got there, that Finian was coming later on and I smiled, aware that I was happy sitting on this bus on my own, blue Joni Mitchell dress, beat up cowboy boots, my body light and comfortable, returning the conductor's smile every time he passed by me.

Despite the sun outside, the flat was chilly, bare looking, now that we were both packed, Ethna's bed stripped, no trace of her left, probably sitting in the dining car eating a hearty meal.

"Well wee Logue, we're nearly there," Maeve in high spirits handing me a cigarette.

We opened back the double doors, letting in light and heat from the bedroom window, still missing the two-bar heater.

"What time's Finian gonna be here?" I really didn't fancy him anymore.

"I'm not sure, he was calling to some fella in Crumlin who has a set of uilleann pipes for sale, it'll probably be after 6."

"I hope he has money for food, I've only the money Ethna gave me for the landlord, I'll write a cheque for the aul' bollocks."

"Finian's bound to have money from the gig last night, anyway I've a wee bit over from my grant, we'll not starve."

"There's a drop of milk left, I'll make us a cup of tea." I put a small saucepan of water on the gas and rinsed out cups under the cold water tap, drying them with toilet roll stolen from college. It was time to tell her about the 'Sunday World' scandal. She listened, brown eyes unblinking, refusing to look perturbed or shocked at my dramatisation, me holding back the vital piece of information that no charges would be brought in the case.

"Are you sure they were the cards we sold?" she wasn't giving in easily.

"Definitely, Jesus I nearly died of a heart attack when I saw the photographs, I recognised them immediately, how could I ever forget! All those poor people being conned out of their money" she sold three cards.

"50p isn't a fortune, as far as I know there's some clause that charities only have to donate a small percentage of the money they collect anyway," Miss Clever Clogs.

"Yeah it said something about that at the end of the article, still it made me a bit nervous…" flogging a dead horse.

"I wouldn't worry about it, we're away home tomorrow and Heenan doesn't know our addresses, don't be worrying wee Logue," patronising.

"Do you think Rosie knew the story on those tickets?" hint of a challenge in my voice.

She blinked slowly, lips pursed ruefully, shaking her head "Cathy, I haven't a clue what Rosie knew, she saw us coming, I know that much."

"We were right fucking eejits, weren't we?" why was I not annoyed?

"No, we were just kind, but we won't be as innocent in the future," Maeve wasn't annoyed either.

After that we sat all afternoon waiting, afraid to leave the flat in case Finian called, smoking, chatting, silences.

"This reminds me of times dad was late picking me up from the convent, like Christmas or Easter, everyone else gone home. Jesus it was miserable, the nuns passing every so often giving me that fake sweet smile, nearly glad I was suffering."

"I know, I remember, but mum was nearly always on time, she was good like that." Maeve was lying back on the musty sofa.

"I don't think anyone moved into Rosie's hovel yet," I changed the subject, didn't want to lose my nice, happy feeling.

"It needs to be done up, nobody would live in it the way it is," she pulled a distasteful face.

"That aule bollocks won't do it up; it would kill him to spend the money. I hate having to give him a cheque for £50, I really do" visions of the summer gear in Cassidy's floated, a plan hatching in my brain.

"Do you think I want to give him the last of my grant money, I do like hell." Was she thinking what I was thinking?

"Maeve?"

"What?" her mouth was twisting, trying to block a smile.

"Why don't we keep the money. I'll run over to the Northern Bank now and write a cheque for £50 cash. You can have half of Ethna's money, that'll be £75 each, Jesus what we couldn't do with that," waves of delight overtaking me, please go along with this plan Maeve.

"Will your mother not be suspicious about such a big cheque?"

I nearly had her.

"No way, I'll tell her seeing as you and Ethna were paying cash I didn't want to be odd writing a cheque." Mum would have a fit but what odds.

"We'll need to be away really early tomorrow morning then before Heenan arrives, she was definitely on for it.

"I've a better idea, we'll fuck off outta here this evening as soon as Finian arrives, I can't stick this shithole one more night."

We were on our feet, holding hands, jumping up and down, giggling, shrieking, then saying "Shush, someone might hear us."

"Right wee Logue, run over to the bank, I'll start stripping the beds, check under them, make sure we're leaving nothing behind."

The bank clerk knew me, he seemed a little surprised the cheque was a lot bigger than usual. My heart pounding, watching him counting the new crisp notes. Crossing the road again to 91, breeze blowing through my hair, knowing I would have cool summer clothes for once without having to beg for them. It was too late for Cassidy's but that wasn't a problem. How often had I touched the beautiful clothes in Mod Boutique, Letterkenny, aching to buy their cotton broderie-anglaise dresses and cute towelling halter neck tops, walking out of there angry, frustrated, bumping into girls in the doorway who could afford those treasures. Well not anymore, tomorrow afternoon I would be in trying on, buying what I wanted because I could.

A little after 7 o'clock a dark brown Ford Granada pulled up on the kerb, head of corkscrew curls visible behind the driver's wheel. Desert boots bounding up the steps, Maeve moved before the doorbell rang; I arranged myself on the pink armchair, relaxed pose, cowboy boots dangling on the arm, Joni Mitchell dress spread out, bohemian. He followed Maeve in, sallow complexion, green eyes, still gorgeous, still wearing the pale blue grandfather shirt and faded jeans. My heartbeat remained normal; echoing his smile, feeling sweet relief, I was his equal, ready to be his friend.

"How's about ya, Cathy," throwing himself into the sofa, dust rising into the shaft of sunlight from the bedroom window.

"How's it going Finian?"

Maeve sat beside him glancing urgently at both of us, speaking in a solemn tone.

"Finian how would you feel about driving home this evening, I mean right away? Cathy and me would really like to get outta here tonight," hint of mystery.

Caught off guard he smiled, keeping calm, "Aye, no problem, we'll make The Grill in time for the disco. What's the big rush though?" his eyes began to wander, noticing the bare walls, empty shelves.

No point telling him the Rosie saga, he had detested her, no sympathy waiting there.

"We owe the landlord money and we haven't got it, he's charging us for those drawers we burned on him ages back, do you remember? On top of that we owe him four week's rent," I threw my eyes to heaven.

Producing a ready made joint he began lighting up, sucking the smoke deep into his lungs watching us closely. Maeve took up the cudgels, "and he's a mean aule bollocks, charging big rent for these pigsties, driving around in his big fancy Merc," she took the joint from Finian, my turn next.

"The aule shit even blamed us when we got robbed," I looked up quickly, sorry I mentioned that.

"You got robbed?" he was almost sneering.

"There wasn't much taken," Maeve to the rescue, exhaling, handing me the joint, then remembering "do you want to try Cathy, might be OK now?"

I wanted to, to prove that I could, then declined "No, you're alright, Maeve, just in case," confused look on Finian's face. "Doesn't really agree with me," enough explanation for now.

"So, the landlord is an aule shite, say shite, Cathy, like a good Irish woman," he was stoned. "I think Mr. Shitey deserves a wee calling card before yous leave, a wee thank you to him for providing such nice living quarters and being so good to yous," he sniggered.

"What, like leave a note on the table saying good luck and fuck you?" Maeve liked her idea.

"Ah Jesus McLaughlin, you can do better than that, come on use that brain, be creative," he reached over tapping her forehead with his index finger.

"We'll burn the other bloody sideboard, how about that?" my idea was better.

"Too messy, I'd need a saw and there's probably no firelighters." He was on his feet now pacing, getting into the spirit. "Come on, I'm Charles Manson, you're my women, my family."

"God, we're not going to kill Heenan are we?" Maeve looked appalled.

"Ah would you behave McLaughlin, I mean we'll just disturb his fat head."

"I have a packet of jumbo markers, we'll write creepy, hateful stuff all over the walls, use red a lot and make it look like blood," I was inspired.

"Dead on Logue, ace, get the markers and we'll do this thing," he was dancing with delight.

Maeve's eyes were bloodshot but her thinking was clear "Should we not put our things in the car first, do the place over, then get the hell outta here?" good idea.

Fuelled, we lugged rucksacks, plastic bags, boxes of books, blankets, out to the car, putting them on the back seat. Finian carrying our heavy square cases, fitting them in the boot, returning to the flat, only our shoulder bags left, hanging on the faded pink armchair, once Rosie's throne.

Setting to work, markers in hand, brown, red, orange, no method, no conferring, just a frenzy of slogans, macabre twisted messages. Writing on ancient Victorian walls, moving from sitting room to bedroom, defiling, scarring. DEATH TO PIGS, SATAN RULES, HELTER SKELTER, BURN IN HELL, BLOOD WILL FLOW, TIME TO PAY.

We stood back, reading silently, admiring, smiling and sated.

"One more wee message," Maeve winked, fumbling in her cloth shoulder bag producing a tube of dark red lipstick. She moved to the mirror above the sitting room mantle. YOU WILL DIE! She smudged the edges like wet dripping blood, our final chilling farewell to Mr. Tommy Heenan.

Shoulder bags on, we followed Finian, slamming the door to flat no. 1 for the last time, moving through the hall, a final whiff of squalor, loneliness, and indifference with top notes of urine, desperation and Rosie. The ancient heavy green door to 91 South Circular closed tight behind us. We didn't look back.

Maeve's hand on the front passenger door, mine on the wad of fresh £10 notes inside my crocheted bag, squeezing into the back seat. Dusk was falling, we pulled away from the footpath driving into traffic, streetlights coming on, lighting cigarettes, each in our own separate heaven. Finian pushed in the cassette winking at me in the rear-view mirror. J.J. Cale sang "After midnight we're gonna let it all hang out…" and I winked back.

END